Francis B. Nyamnjoh
Stories from Abakwa
Mind Searching
The Disillusioned African
The Convert
Souls Forgotten
Married But Available

Dibussi Tande
No Turning Back. Poems of Freedom 1990-1993

Kangsen Feka Wakai
Fragmented Melodies

Ntemfac Ofege
Namondo. Child of the Water Spirits
Hot Water for the Famous Seven

Emmanuel Fru Doh
Not Yet Damascus
The Fire Within
Africa's Political Wastelands: The Bastardization of
Cameroon

Thomas Jing
Tale of an African Woman

Peter Wuteh Vakunta
Grassfields Stories from Cameroon
Green Rape: Poetry for the Environment
Majunga Tok: Poems in Pidgin English
Cry, My Beloved Africa
No Love Lost

Ba'bila Mutia
Coils of Mortal Flesh

Kehbuma Langmia
Titabet and the Takumbeng

Victor Elame Musinga
The Barn
The Tragedy of Mr. No Balance

Ngessimo Mathe Mutaka
Building Capacity: Using TEFL and African
Languages as Development-oriented Literacy Tools

Milton Krieger
Cameroon's Social Democratic Front: Its History and
Prospects as an Opposition Political Party, 1990-2011

Sammy Oke Akombi
The Raped Amulet
The Woman Who Ate Python
Beware the Drives: Book of Verse

Susan Nkwentie Nde
Precipice

Francis B. Nyamnjoh &
Richard Fonteh Akum
The Cameroon GCE Crisis: A Test of Anglophone
Solidarity

Joyce Ashuntantang & Dibussi Tande

Their Champagne Party Will End! Poems in Honor of
Bate Besong

Emmanuel Achu
Disturbing the Peace

Rosemary Ekosso
The House of Falling Women

Peterkins Manyong
God the Politician

George Ngwane
The Power in the Writer: Collected Essays on Culture,
Democracy & Development in Africa

John Percival
The 1961 Cameroon Plebiscite: Choice or Betrayal

Albert Azeyeh
Réussite scolaire, faillite sociale : généalogie mentale
de la crise de l'Afrique noire francophone

Aloysius Ajab Amin & Jean-Luc Dubois
Croissance et développement au Cameroun :
d'une croissance équilibrée à un développement
équitable

Carlson Anyangwe
Imperialistic Politics in Cameroun:
Resistance & the Inception of the Restoration of the
Statehood of Southern Cameroons

Bill F. Ndi
K'Cracy, Trees in the Storm and Other Poems

Kathryn Toure, Therese Mungah
Shalo Tchombe & Thierry Karsenti
ICT and Changing Mindsets in Education

Charles Alobwed'Epie
The Day God Blinked

G.D. Nyamndi
Babi Yar Symphony

Samuel Ebelle Kingue
Si Dieu était tout un chacun de nous?

Ignasio Malizani Jimu
Urban Appropriation and Transformation: bicycle,
taxi and handcart operators in Mzuzu, Malawi

Justice Nyo' Wakai:
Under the Broken Scale of Justice: The Law and
My Times

No Love Lost

Peter Wuteh Vakunta

Langaa Research & Publishing CIG
Mankon, Bamenda

Publisher:
Langaa RPCIG
(*Langaa* Research & Publishing Common Initiative Group)
P.O. Box 902 Mankon
Bamenda
North West Province
Cameroon
Langaagrp@gmail.com
www.langaapublisher.com

Distributed outside N. America by African Books Collective
orders@africanbookscollective.com
www.africanbookscollective.com

Distributed in N. America by Michigan State University Press
msupress@msu.edu
www.msupress.msu.edu

ISBN:9956-558-40-0

© Peter Wuteh Vakunta 2009
First published 2009

DISCLAIMER

DEDICATION

For the literati of Ongola

The committed writer knows that speech is action: he knows that to reveal is to change and that one cannot reveal except by planning to change. [Pascal Kyoore, 1996]

1

When Tewuh received his Bachelor of Science degree from the hands of the Vice-Chancellor of the University of Ongola, he said to himself that those years of hardship were over. He had worked very hard and it had paid off. Smiling from ear to ear he hugged and shook hands with his relatives who had come to see him graduate. Every member of his family was present at the commencement ceremony. Even his 90-year-old grandmother, enfeebled by Parkinson's disease, was in attendance.

"I thank you my child. Thank you very much for making me proud today. Who wouldn't be proud to have a son like you? You can call the white man's book and speak through your nostrils like the white man. I am a very proud old woman today," the haggard woman said, hugging her grandson.

"It is all because of you, granny. You did your best to see me grow up," Tewuh said, holding her emaciated arms.

"If Nyi Almighty King of the Skies called me today, I would hold my head high and go to meet him," the old woman said, holding her grandson in her bony hands.

When the ceremony was over, Tewuh went home in the company of his jubilant relatives and friends. Dressed in a black three-piece suit and a pair of black leather shoes, the 20-year-old boy led the homebound procession, holding his diploma in his muscular hands. He gallivanted on stubby legs and winked at the young ladies in the crowd as if to seduce them. His friends kept badgering him with questions about his future career.

"Bo, di kana big book wey you don get'am so no bi you go daso be na djintete for dis kontri?"[1] Bunda, his childhood friend asked.

"Massa, lef me da big book palava. Mek we daso go dance makossa den dammer for long,"[2] he responded trying to be evasive.

"Ni Tewuh, mek you no forget me taim wey you dong jandre-oh. You sabi say taim wey youa broda dey for ontop plum stick you go chop sweet plum, no?"[3] one of the girls said, winking at him.

"You tok na true tok, sista,"[4] Tewuh responded.

When they reached home, his father asked him an unexpected question.

"This big certificate of yours will open all kinds of doors for you on the job market, isn't that right, my son?"

The sexagenarian hadn't said a word since they set out on the return journey from Nkulunlun. Sixty miles separated them from the village of Lohmeukoh. If they had a car, it would have taken them less than an hour to get home. Hiring a taxi would have meant spending a whole year's income from their farm produce. They had to walk home.

"Papa, with a certificate like this I will be able to work in any office I want in this country," the young man said confidently. He was very proud of his achievement. He had worked very hard to earn his degree.

"We praise God for giving you to us," Nah Mbiah said, beaming. The boy's mother was full of excitement.

It was pitch dark outside when they got home. They were tired but happy. An illustrious son of the soil had just returned with a great booty. Tewuh's father, who equated his son's achievement to killing a lion, had bought a five-year-old cow and two goats for his son's graduation party. The very day his son had set foot in the white man's school, it had dawned on him that one day he would come back like a hero. Tewuh's mother aided by other female members of the family had cooked basketsful of delicious food: fufu and njama-njama soup, koki and ripe plantains, ero and water-fufu, calabar yams, kwa-coco, and egusi soup. There was alcohol galore: majunga, jobajo, odontol, matango, nkang, kwacha, mbu, fofo and palm-wine. They ate and danced to favorite makossa and magangbeu tunes till dawn.

Tewuh woke up the following morning feeling ill at ease. In the midst of the excitement, he had not given thought to how he would get to Yaoundé in order to apply for a job. To apply for a job he had to travel to the nation's capital. All applicants were required to personally submit their applications at the Ministry of the Public Service and be interviewed there. Yaoundé was some 2200 miles away from home. He couldn't cover that distance on foot. He needed the sum of 10.000 CFA francs to pay his fare. He didn't have the money. Worse still, he knew nobody in the capital city.

"Where will I live during my job search in Yaoundé?" the boy asked his father.

~ 2 ~

"When you get to Yaoundé, try your best to find Chui Bah's son. His parents live in this village. He'll give you a bed to sleep on. A tribesman is a brother," his father said, giving him the sum of 11.000 CFA francs.

"Papa, I don't know Chui Bah's son," Tewuh said, looking confused.

"Chui Bah's son is called Londu. He speaks the same language as you do. Go see him and ask for help," his father said, stroking his graying beard.

"Papa, Yaoundé is a big city. How am I going to find Londu in a huge city like that?"

"Oh, don't worry. He looks like his father. He is short and stout. When he comes to see his father and mother, he always wears a blue suit, a pair of brown leather shoes and a gold watch. You can't miss him," the old man said confidently.

"Papa, hundreds of men wear blue suits, brown leather shoes, and gold watches in Yaoundé. How am I going to pick out Londu from this crowd?"

"Well, you'll have to try hard to find your tribesman. Remember that the woman that never tried hard enough to fall pregnant died childless," Nah Mbiah said.

"I will try my best, Nah," Tewuh said.

"Travel well, my son," his mother said.

"Go, my son. May the gods of our ancestors show you the straight road. May they open friendly doors for you," his father said, holding his son close to his hairy chest.

They were standing at the Amour Mezam motor park. Suddenly, he let go his son and walked briskly away without looking back. He did not want him to see his tears.

"Stay well, Papa," Tewuh said, waving at his father.

"Go well, my son," his mother said in a broken voice looking pitifully at her son. Tears stood in her panther eyes.

"Travel well, son. May the ground rise to meet you, and may the wind always be behind you," his father said, wishing the boy a safe trip.

The trip to Yaoundé lasted several hours. Tewuh was at his wits' end when the bus screeched to a halt at the Ndobolo bus station at *Carrefour* Obili[5]. The beehive activity in the city confused him. Yellow cabs sped past at the speed of lightening. Infuriated taxi drivers hauled insults at one another. To Tewuh's surprise, two taximen who had been pointing their index fingers into the air as a response to provocation, suddenly stopped the engines of their cars, jumped out and got into a fist-fight.

"*Tu think que tu es même quoi?*" One of the drivers said to his offender.

"*Et toi tu member say tu es sorti de la cuisse du Jupiter, non?*" the other responded.

"Youa mami pima!"[6] the other said, slapping him in the face.

"*Die dog! Ne me touche pas again!*"[7] the other said, grabbing the aggressor by the collar.

Tewuh heard passengers inside both taxis screaming in French. He could hardly understand what they were saying.

As he wondered how he was going to find Londu, he heard passersby speaking in languages he had never heard before. He felt like a pygmy in the land of giants. He prayed that some one would speak *Meukoh*, his native tongue. People scurried in various directions as though their homes were on fire. How on earth was he going to find Londu in this maze? Placing his traveling bag between his legs, he stood at the bus station arms across his broad chest, feeling like a fish out of water.

Suddenly, an idea crossed his mind. He decided to look for his tribesman in bars and nightclubs in the vicinity. He looked at his watch. It was 8:00pm. He slung his bag across his shoulders, and walked into the city center. The first night-club he arrived at was called Biabia Nite Club. It was full of wolowoss[8] on the lookout for clients. He went in, bought a bottle of jobajo,[9] and sat at a vacant table next to the DJ. Skinny girls wearing see-through outfits and high-heels were gyrating on the dance floor. Men and women chattered in French, a language that sounded like Chinese to Tewuh. He had dropped French in secondary school when his arrogant Francophone teacher called him a mbut[10] when he got a grade of "C" on his finals because he could not conjugate the verb *être*[11] in French. How he hated that man!

He was still wondering how to find Londu as he watched the merrymakers hover around him.

"You want maboya for the nite, cheri coco? *Je suis propre*, no HIV."[12]

Startled, Tewuh got out of his daydream. A fair complexioned girl with abundant hair and breasts like pumpkins stood over him wriggling her semi-nude protruding buttocks. She looked like a teenager.

"No, sista. I no di fain woman. I di fain ma kontryman wey yi deh for dis town,"[13] Tewuh responded looking straight into her blue eyes.

"Wheti be name for youa kontryman"[14] the harlot inquired.

"Londu. He commot for Meka village."[15]

"You commot for Meka you self-self?"[16]

"Yes, I be Meka pikin meself-self."[17]

"I mimba say I sabi da Londu wey you de fain'am."[18]

"Na true tok you de tok? So you sabi ma kontryman!"[19]

"Yes, Londu na taximan, no?"[20]

"I no sabi de kana wok wey yi de wok, sista."[21]

"Ah yo mba, eh! See me some man. You de fain person wey you no sabi'am?"[22]

"Sista, I commot for Bamenda just now, just now. I come na for fain wok for ya. Ma repe say if I reach mek I fain Londu."[23]

"Bo, give man one jobajo, no. I go fain Londu gee you."[24]

"Wheti you de shark no, sista?"[25]

"No be daso 33 Export?"[26]

Tewuh bought her a bottle of 33 Export beer. She used her teeth to open the bottle, drank half of it at a go, and slammed the bottle on the table in front of him.

"I de come ma broda"[27], she said and walked out of the nightclub, swaying from one side to the other like a model competing in a beauty contest.

She didn't tell Tewuh where she was going. He thought she had gone for good. After an hour she reappeared in the company of a short heavily built man in his mid-thirties. He was clean-shaven and dressed in black leather trousers and jacket. His polished black leather shoes and gold watch glittered in the dim lights of the nightclub.

"Na youa kontryman dis,"[28] the girl said, pointing at the newcomer.

"I am Londu. I hear you're looking for me?"

"Yes, I am Tewuh. Nice to meet you, brother Londu. I come from Meka. I'm son of Pa Kunta."

"Oh, nice to meet you," Londu said, stretching his right hand to greet Tewuh.

"My father asked me to look for you when I get here."

"Ah, is that right? I have been to the village a couple of times but haven't met you."

"Yes, that's because I was away in college."

"I see. So what brings you to the nation's capital?"

"Job search, my brother. I have just graduated from college and need a job."

"Congratulations!" What did you study in college?"

"Plant science, I have a degree in plant science."

"Great! Let's go home," Londu said, leading his tribesman out of the busy nightclub, after buying two beers for the young lady who had introduced him to Tewuh.

The two young men were now sitting on a couch in Londu's two-bedroom flat in the Madagascar neighborhood. Tewuh took a quick look at a leather bag sitting on a mahogany table in the north end of the room. It was full of small plastic bags containing some white powdery stuff. Foreign currencies lay pell-mell on the table: euro, pound, dollar, yen, naira, cedi, and rand.

"Do you smoke?" Londu asked, offering Tewuh a pack of Benson and Hedges.

"No, thanks," he said.

"Do you want something to eat?" Londu asked.

"Yes, thanks brother. I am starving," Tewuh said, hardly believing the generosity of this man he was meeting for the first time.

Londu quickly prepared a bowl of corn-fufu[29] and fried bunga[30] while his visitor read a copy of the *Cameroon Post* weekly that lay on the center table. When the meal was ready Londu washed his hands and both men attacked the lumps of food each with his five fingers.

"Massa, you cook like a woman! The food is so tasty!" Tewuh said.

"Thank you. If nkwankanda no sabi cook no be yi go die hungry,"[31] Londu said without lifting his head from the bowl of fufu.

"You said you've come to look for a job?"

"Yes."

"Do you have money?"

"No, I don't. I am fresh out of college. My father gave me just enough to pay my fare to Yaoundé," Tewuh said.

"You don't have money, and yet you want a job? That's impossible!" Londu said, laughing uproariously.

"What's impossible?" Tewuh asked.

"Getting a job here without money," Londu said.

"I don't understand," Tewuh said, shaking his clean-shaven head in disbelief.

"Believe it or not, it takes money and connections to get a job here," Londu said.

"Why?" Tewuh asked.

"That's because you have to grease the palm of everyone that handles your job application file, including the *planton*. That's the way things work here," Londu said.

"Who is *planton*?"

"The planton is the office messenger who transports files from office to office."

"Are you serious?"

"Oh yes!" Here in Yaoundé, the *planton* is the boss; he's even more important than the real boss."

"God forbid bad thing!"[32] Tewuh exclaimed.

"God is on vacation in Yaoundé, my friend! It doesn't matter what kind of degree you have. You have to tchoko[33] if you want a job," Londu explained.

"I'm lost. I've spent four years working hard to earn a degree and you're telling me it doesn't matter?"

"That's the bitter truth, brother."

"If a degree doesn't matter on the job market, what does?" Tewuh asked opening and closing his lips like a fish.

"Do you speak French?

"No."

"That makes things worse, my friend!" Londu added.

"Why?"

"Everyone here speaks French. This is the territory of Francophones."

"So?"

"If you don't understand French, you're a persona non grata in this part of the country. They will call you mon Bamenda.[34] Others will call you Anglo[35] and poke fun at you everywhere you go," Londu said.

"Is that real?"

"Take it from me, my brother. The marriage between Francophones and Anglophones in Ongola [36] is one of convenience," Londu said, falling asleep.

Tewuh woke up the following day feeling stressed out. The question of having to give bribes in order to get a job had kept him wide awake all night. The language question frightened him even more.

"Use this to pay your taxi fare to the Public Service Ministry. I'm leaving for work."

"Thank you very much, bro," Tewuh said, taking the 500 CFA francs bill from Londu.

"My girlfriend will show you where to catch a taxi to the Ministry. She will be here in a few minutes," Londu said, leaving the house.

Tewuh jumped into his khaki trousers, a marine blue long-sleeved shirt and black shoes. Soon a young woman came in and introduced herself as Clotide. She accompanied him to the taxi rank, showed him where to stand and flag down yellow taxis and left for her tailoring shop. He had been standing there for close to thirty minutes when a taxi screeched to a halt in front of him.

"Please, drop me at the Ministry of the Public Service," he said to the driver.

"*Fils de chien! T'es malade?*[37]" the driver yelled at him, taking off at the speed of lightening.

Five other taxis went past him without stopping. He felt too humiliated to flag down a cab. The sixth one stopped.

"I am going to the Public Service Ministry, please drop me there," he said.

"*Anglo! Fiche-le camp, idiot! Va te faire porter par ta maman!*" [38]the taxi driver hollered.

"What in the world is going on?" Tewuh asked himself.

By reading the body language of the taxi drivers he concluded that they were hurling insults at him. He stared wide-eyed at taxis passing, wondering why they were not picking him up. Did they understand him? Were they being spiteful? The word "Anglo" thrown at him by one of the taximen reminded him of what Londu had told him the night before. Crestfallen, he decided to walk five miles to the Ministry. The morning sun was getting hot and he was sweating profusely as he walked. If he had a job, he would forget this humiliation. As he wove his way through the rush-hour traffic, he dreamed of the day when he would own his own car. It would be an SUV, nothing more nothing less. He would show these bastards that he is a bachelors' degree holder. He would buy himself a house too. Owning a house in the nation's capital would be a dream come true. In his reverie, he covered the five miles without realizing it. The oval building of the Public Service Ministry stood in front of him. He walked straight into it.

"Good morning Madam," he said to a receptionist sitting at the information desk.

"*Monsieur, je ne comprends pas votre dialecte-là, hein!*"[39] The coquettish young woman replied without looking at Tewuh. She was busy applying lipstick on her bulbous lips.

"I beg your pardon?" Tewuh said, looking straight into her green eyes.

"*Ici c'est Yaoundé, you ya. Il faut parler français, monsieur. On ne parle que le français ici*,"[40] the woman spoke at the top of her voice without taking her eyes off her mirror.

Tewuh took a few steps backwards and walked quietly out of the office, feeling frustrated. Everyone around him spoke French. On his way out, he saw a door that was ajar. He walked through it and found himself in a large hall filled with people quarreling over files. There were about fifty people in there, most of them men in their mid-twenties. He decided to approach one of the men.

"Good morning, sir."

"*Quoi?*"[41] the man responded looking at him as if he'd just landed from a strange planet.

"I said good morning, sir," Tewuh repeated.

"You come for Bamenda?" one man asked, laughing up his sleeve.

"What did you say, sir?" Tewuh asked, a frown on his doll-like face.

"*C'est un Biafrais*,"[42] the man said, spitting in his face.

The whole hall burst out into thundering laughter.

Tewuh had had it. He walked up to his aggressor who was dressed in faded blue jeans and a black shirt, grabbed him by the collar, lifted him off the ground, and threw him on the bare cement floor, *pwam!*

"Gentleman, I am not a dog! I am a human being like you! You don't treat me like dirt!" he said, looking at the hostile faces in the hall like a wounded lion.

The man he had thrown down got up and gave him a quick kick in his private parts. Tewuh lost consciousness and fell to the ground. When he regained consciousness he found himself in a hospital ward at the *Hôpital central de Yaoundé*.[43] Londu was sitting beside him on the bed where he was lying.

"My girlfriend informed me of the problem you had at the Ministry this morning. She said you were brought here in an ambulance when she called the police. Are you feeling better?" Londu asked.

"Yes, I'm feeling better," Tewuh answered, showing his friend the injuries he'd sustained on his testicles as a result of the scuffle.

"I advise you to return to the village as soon as you get well," Londu said.

"Why?"

"I believe that your degree will be put to better use over there in Abakwa."

"You think so?" Tewuh asked, tears welling in his bloodshot eyes.

"Yes. Don't waste your time here. It is a dead end for people like you who can't speak the French language."

"I see. So it is French or nothing."

"More or less, this place is a burial ground for most Anglophones," Londu said, shaking his head.

Two weeks later, Tewuh left the *Hôpital central*.

"Take this my friend and pay your way back home," Londu said, giving him two 10,000 CFA franc bills.

"Brother, I can't thank you enough. May God repay your kindness tenfold," Tewuh said, taking the money.

"Good luck in your new job search! Remember that this city is a torture chamber for educated people like you," Londu said, waving his tribesman goodbye at the Tchatchou motor Park in *quartier* Melen.

Tewuh arrived at home that same day in the evening. His father had left for his cassava farm situated one hundred miles away from the village. He entered his room, flung himself on the bed and went into deep slumber.

2

The following morning Tewuh did not feel rested. He had battled incessantly the whole night.

"I won't let you go! Come along now!" she said, baring the tobacco-stained teeth beneath her thick lips. Terrified, the boy stared into her hooded eyes. He feared he was going to die and decided to put up a fight. His thin lips quivered as he threw his hands around the elephantine body of the haggard-looking octogenarian.

"Leave me alone!" Who are you? What do you want from me? Go away!" Tewuh shouted, struggling to escape from the phantom's strangulating grip. She burst into thunderous laughter, exposing her charcoal black gums.

"You don't know me, little one?"

"I don't know you! Get away from me!" the boy shouted again.

"I'll tell you who I am. I am your father's great grandmother, little one."

"You're my father's great grandmother?"

"Yes!"

"Go away, you old witch! My father's great grandmother died many years ago. I never met her. Go away! You're not my father's great grandmother!" Tewuh screamed breathlessly.

"Today is your turn, little one. Don't try to fight back. I have come for you. I will kill you! I will destroy all the books you read. Come follow me, now!"

Tewuh gasped for breath when he woke up. Cold sweat ran all over his ebony body. He had been dreaming. It was a nightmare. When he recounted his dream to his mother, she did not believe him.

"You're making this up," his mother said when he told her about the fight he had had with his great grandmother in a dream.

"The Bible warns us against superstition. Your great grandmother cannot appear to you in a dream. I believe the Prince of Darkness is trying to build his kingdom in you, my son," Nah Mbiah said, looking at her son in disbelief.

"Nah, what do you mean? I am telling you that I had a bad dream last night, and you say the Prince of Darkness is building his kingdom in me? What is that supposed to mean?" Tewuh asked angrily.

"My son, let's not fight. When your house is burning you don't wait for others to put out the fire. Let's go to Father McMahon," she said.

"What will Father McMahon do?"

"Let's go and tell your story to the white man of God. He may find a solution to this problem," she said, wiping a tear from her squinting eyes.

"Nah, I will not go to Father McMahon. What do I need from him? Does he interpret dreams?" Tewuh protested.

"No, he is not an interpreter of dreams but he may pray for a solution to your problem," his mother insisted.

"What do prayers have to do with bad dreams?" Tewuh asked, raising his voice. He slammed the door of his mother's two bedroom mud hut in which they were sitting and went to see his father. Pa Kunta invited his son into the living room of his three-bedroom house built out of sun dried bricks.

"Sit down here," he said, pointing to a vacant cane-chair beside his bamboo bed.

"Did you sleep well, Papa?" Tewuh greeted.

"Yes, my night was peaceful, and how was yours? You look worried. How was your journey to Yaoundé? You came back so soon. Is there a problem?" the man asked, scratching his balding head.

"Yes, Papa I had a terrible dream last night," Tewuh said.

"A terrible dream?"

"Yes, Papa, I dreamed a bad dream."

"What happened in your dream, my son?"

"I was attacked by a very old woman. She was dressed in a white gown and held a machete in her right hand."

"Was she trying to kill you?"

"Yes Papa, she said she wanted to kill me and destroy all my books. From time to time, she would raise the weapon above my head, threatening to cut me into pieces if I did not follow her immediately."

"Follow her where?"

"She did not say where."

"Is that true, my son?"

"Yes, Papa."

"Did you recognize the woman?"

"No, Papa. But I remember what she said."

"What did she say?"

"She said she was your great grandmother."

"Oh! My ancestors! Help! What offense have I committed?"

Pa Kunta was shaking like a dry leaf in the harmattan wind when he led his son into his wife's hut. Have you heard this?" he asked, sitting down on a stool reserved for him by the fireside.

"Are you talking about our son's dream?"

"Yes, that's what I am talking about."

"Yes, he talked to me about it. What are we going to do?"

"We are going to appease our ancestors."

"How are we going to do that?"

"There's only one way of appeasing our ancestors."

"And what's that?"

"We've got to pour libation. Our ancestors are unhappy. When the dead are angry, it's an indication that the gods are angry."

"So what?" Nah Mbiah asked disdainfully.

"The right thing to do when the ancestors are angry is to pour libation," Pa Kunta said.

"What are you talking about? What has a child got to do with pagan practices?" Nah Mbiah asked, biting her thin lips.

"Woman, shut up! What are you calling pagan practices?" her husband shouted.

"The thing you call libation! This child goes to a Catholic church, yet you want to drag him into superstition just because he has had a bad dream," the woman retorted.

"Woman, if I hear a single word from that big mouth of yours again, I will roast a stone and make you sit on it, do you hear me? You refer to the customs of my forefathers as superstition! Youa head correct?"[44]

"Yes, my head is correct. That's why I don't worship idols!"

"Woman, I have heard enough of your nonsense," Pa Kunta said, striking his wife in the face with his left hand.

Nah Mbiah fell down from the bamboo chair on which she was sitting and cried like a baby. Her nostrils oozed blood. Unperturbed by the act of abuse he had just committed, Pa Kunta fell on his wife, grabbed her head in both his hands, and kept hitting it against the hearthstones. Tewuh was very angry. He got up and pulled his father off his mother and asked her to run for her life. She did not run away. She threw herself on her husband, got

~ 13 ~

hold of his testicles, and kept pulling hard at them. The man roared like a wounded lion and kicked her in the groin. She fell and fainted.

The following morning Pa Kunta summoned every member of his lineage to his compound. Everyone came, the young and the old; men and women; cousins and second-cousins. Tewuh's mother alone was absent. After learning that she had escaped to her parents' compound, some relatives advised Pa Kunta to go and fetch her. Others dissuaded him, pointing out that it was taboo for a woman to make derogatory remarks about ancestral worship.

"How could a mother of five abandon her marital home simply because her husband had given her a few beatings in order to correct her mistakes?" Pa Kunta's elder brother asked.

"She erred. Did our forebears not say that the basket of advice is never full?" Bitie, Pa Kunta's cousin asked.

When the audience was quiet, Pa Kunta welcomed them.

"Brothers and sisters, I thank you all for being here today. I thank the gods of our ancestors for bringing you all from your various homes to this compound safely. We ask them to watch over us as we do the thing that they commanded us to do in times of trouble."

No one interrupted him. They all nodded in approbation.

"Our son Tewuh has been having terrible dreams lately," he continued. The dreadful thing is that in his dreams he puts up a fight with my own great grandmother!"

"Aago! Aago! Aago!"[45] the crowd exclaimed.

"You all know that when a child fights with an ancestor in a dream, that is a sign of worse things to come. We must stop the impending fire from consuming us all," Pa Kunta said, facing his assembled relatives.

"Ngieekeuleh! Ngieekeuleh![46]

From his living room, he brought out a black rooster, a jug of palm-wine, a bag of kola nuts, a basketful of smoked mudfish, and a calabash of palm-oil. All present changed into sackcloth made out of raffia fiber and smeared their faces, arms and legs with camwood. Women wore red headscarves; men were bare-headed. They stood in a circle surrounding Pa Kunta, the libation priest. Sixty pairs of eyes watched every gesture he made. He was stark naked except for a multicolored loincloth worn around his broad waist. His porch-marked body was spattered with ground white clay from head to toe. Slung over his muscular shoulders was a goat-skin bag containing the horn of a buffalo, several cowries, and seven feathers of an owl.

"Brothers and sisters, the dead are not dead. We do not see them but they see us," Pa Kunta said, facing his assembled relatives.

"Ngieekeuleh! Ngieekeuleh! they chorused.

"They're in our midst. They talk to us in many ways," he added, fastening two porcupine quills to his *ndikong*[47] hat as he spoke.

"Ngieekeuleh! Ngieekeuleh! they answered with one voice.

"Our ancestors knew better when they said that a single hand cannot tie a bundle. I'll add my voice to theirs by saying that one house cannot make a compound."

"Wuulee, Wuulee, Wuulee!"[48] the crowd shouted again.

"Brothers and sisters, dreams are like streams that reflect our shadows. When you see a giant rat running about in broad daylight, be sure that someone is after its life," he said.

"Wuulee, Wuulee, Wuulee!"they chorused.

"When a child dreams a bad dream and fights with an ancestor, we must appease that ancestor."

"Wuulee, Wuulee, Wuulee!"the crowd roared again.

"How do we appease dead people?" Bunkwe asked.

"By feeding them," Pa Kunta said.

"How do we feed dead people? Bunkwe interrupted again.

"By pouring libation," Pa Kunta answered without looking at him.

"Wuulee, Wuulee, Wuulee!" the people responded in unison.

Bunkwe was Pa Kunta's younger brother who had spent twenty-seven years in the white man's land reading all kinds of books. He had returned home and was having a hard time embracing some aspects of his people's culture. After a while, Bunkwe withdrew from the gathering and walked straight out of the compound without looking back. Nobody tried to stop him. They simply stared at him in dismay.

Pa Kunta invited the audience to accompany him to his great grandmother's grave located in front of his house. He closed his eyes and suddenly went into a trance. Silence fell on the crowd. No one moved. They watched starry-eyed. After a long while, he opened his eyes. Arms akimbo, he uttered inaudible incantations as if to himself. He shut his eyes again, and spat on the dust surrounding the grave. He opened his eyes, did a few dance steps around it, grabbed the rooster by its legs and swung it nine times in the air before wringing its neck with his bare hands. He then intoned the Ndonyi[49] :

> Beuh nyi meukoh
> Ho! ho! Ho ha!
> Fon cheumbe! Ha ho ha!
> Fon ngombi! Ha Ho!
> Fon ngombu! Ho ho! ha ha!
> Fon ngoketunjia! Ho ha! Ho ha!
> Bah teu hah fia keughoh bi! Ho ho ho!
> Beuh nyi meukoh! Hum hum hum!
> Bi chi ba keuhoh bweubelo! Hum hum hum!
> Bi soheu sheu yah! Ho ho hum hum!
> Bi boh yobeu mbweu bah! Ho ha ho!
> Ho ha! ho! Ndonyi!

When the singing was over, Pa Kunta tore the rooster into two equal halves and sprinkled its blood on his great grandmother's grave. He murmured some more incantations and started to run like an insane person to the four corners of the compound, pointing the dead rooster to the west, east, south, and north. He danced, shaking his broad shoulders and wriggling his stiff buttocks.

Suddenly, he stopped, took hold of the jug of palm-wine, and poured its content into his ndeuh mbeuh[50]. After drinking the wine he spat it over the heads of everyone standing in the crowd. Then he intoned a propitiatory prayer song addressed to the ancestors:

> Fathers of our fathers,
> Fathers of our grandfathers,
> Mothers of our mothers,
> Mothers of our grandmothers,
> Here we are today,
> Children of your great grandchildren,
> We are gathered here to salute you,
> Here we are today gathered to pay our respects,
> We are assembled here today,
> To ask for your protection against evil,
> Against witches, and wizards,
> Here we are today reunited,

To ask for your protection,
Against witchcraft; against ill-health,
May you have pity on us, who have offended you,
May you pardon us, who have neglected you,
May you smile on us, who have honored you,
May you watch over us day and night,
Give us more children,
Give our children jobs,
In the offices at Tisong,
Give us more crops,
Give us more rain,
Give us more sun,
Give us more roosters and hens,
Give us long life!

"Wuulee, Wuulee, Wuulee!" members of the audience chorused.

Pa Kunta rolled away the burial stone that lay on his great grandmother's grave. Then he took his cup, filled it with palm-wine, and poured it into the grave saying:

"Mother, take this and drink it. This is the cup of wine given to you by your children and grandchildren. May it become for you the symbolic drink of lasting friendship."

He passed the cup around for everyone to take a sip.

Then he took the clay pot filled with smoked fish steeped in red palm-oil and said:

"Mother, take it and eat it. This is food given by your children and grandchildren. May it serve as lasting nourishment for you and all our ancestors." He passed the clay pot around for everyone to eat a fish.

It was pitch dark outside when Pa Kunta ate the last fish. He thanked his relatives again for leaving their various chores to be part of this very important act of communion. Everyone went home happy and at peace with themselves. That night, Tewuh slept like a log. No dreams, no fights.

3

The next day he decided to go meet his uncle Bunkwe to seek his advice on what to do to get a job. His reasoning was that because his uncle had spent several years in the white man's land and had worked in all kinds of offices there, he would surely have some words of wisdom for him. Small papa, as he usually called him, lived and worked in Garinsabo, a farflung village on the border between Nigeria and the Republic of Ongola.

Soon after his return from overseas with a doctorate degree in veterinary medicine, he had been invited to Yaoundé by the Minister of Fisheries and Animal Husbandry and employed to work as a government delegate for animal husbandry for the Extreme North-West Province. That was during the good old days under the regime of President Baba Toura when a university degree was considered a degree.

"Papa, I'd like to go and see small papa in Garinsabo," Tewuh said, sitting down on a wooden stool in front of his father's fireside.

"Is that so, my son?" his father asked.

"Yes papa," he said.

"Did you sleep well, my son? You look tired."

"My night was peaceful."

"Was yours calm too?"

"Very calm; I slept well. The only thing that bothers me is your inability to find a job," the old man said and sighed.

"Don't worry papa, God is in control. He has plans for me," Tewuh said.

"I can't stop worrying, son. We sent you to university to learn the white man's book, get a good job and help us." The man said, filling his pipe with tobacco.

"I understand papa. I know how you and mami[51] struggled to pay my fees in school, yet I can't find a job with a degree in my pocket," Tewuh said, crestfallen.

"Cry not my son. A banana that will ripen, will do so even if you put it inside cold water," Pa Kunta said, taking out a bottle of snuff from the chest pocket of his threadbare *jumpa*.[52]

"Papa, I am worried about you. At this age I should be earning a salary and taking care of you and my mother," Tewuh said.

"That's true, but if the gods don't give you something, you can't take it by force. There's nothing a man can do against the wish of *Nyi*," the old man said, putting some snuff into his nostrils.

He sneezed noisily and called the name of his father. Taking out an old piece of cloth from his chest pocket he cleaned the wet snuff that had come out of his nose and dropped on his *jumpa*.

"Papa I don't believe it's *Nyi* who is refusing to give me a job," Tewuh said.

"I hear you, child. Those people who live on the other side of the Mungo River don't like us. That's why they wouldn't give our children jobs," he said.

"They want us dead, papa. They tried to kill me in Yaoundé lately," Tewuh said, shedding a tear at the thought of the mishap that had befallen him in the nations's capital.

"*Quifon ne tuh*! *Fon ngombu* [53] will not allow that to happen!" his father exclaimed.

"God cares papa; but human beings don't," Tewuh said in frustration.

"I will let you go to Garinsabo. But let me say this to you: my brother has forgotten our customs. Listen to what he has to say. Take his advice and turn it in your head several times before taking a decision," his father said.

"I hear you papa. Thank you," Tewuh said, rising to go.

"Take this. Keep it on your body at all times. It will protect you from people with four eyes [54]," Pa Kunta said, giving his son a gris-gris [55] sewn in the skin of a leopard.

"Papa, I don't think I really need this. God will protect me," Tewuh protested.

"Take it, this was given to me by my father, peace be upon him. I am giving it to you because I love you. Keep it in your pocket wherever you go," Pa Kunta said, putting the talisman in the boy's right palm.

As soon as Tewuh left his father, he went straight to his mother's hut to wish her goodbye.

"Travel well, son. Has your father given you money to pay your fare?" she asked.

"Yes, mami. I have enough money to pay my way," Tewuh said, hugging his mother.

"Go well. May God Almighty and his angels guide you day and night,"Nah Mbiah said.

"Good bye, mami."

Tewuh left his mother and went to Abakwa to board a taxi for Garinsabo. The mammy-wagon[56] lorry he took had a license plate that read: "God's case no appeal". No sooner had he sat down on one of the wooden benches that served as seats in the vehicle than a woman dressed in a brightly colored outfit got up from where he had been sitting and shouted:

"Ma broda and sista dem, I salute wona in the name of our Lord Jesus Christ,"[57] she said, holding a bible in her left hand.

"Na wich kain barlok dis no? Jesus na who no, Madam?"[58]said a skinny man sitting in the back of the car.

"Wona bad pipo! Repent for the kingdom of God done near!"[59] she shouted at the top of her voice,looking disdainfully at all the passengers.

"Craze pipo dai kain kain-o,"[60] Tewuh said, suppressing a laugh.

"John 3:16," the woman said.

"Madam, wheti you de smoke?"[61] an irate passenger asked.

"For God so loved the world that he gave his only begotten son. That whosover believeth in him should not perish, but have everlasting life," the woman continued.

"Yi de smoke na wee-wee, "[62] another passenger said.

"Blessed are the poor in spirit; for they shall inherit the kingdom of God," she shouted, opening her Bible in the middle where she had put a bookmark.

"Leave us in peace, Madam! We are living in hell in this country. Why preach to us about heaven?" a young man dressed in faded jeans and black agbada[63] said.

"Man shall not live by bread alone; but by every word that comes out of the mouth of God," the woman said, trying to read from the Bible.

"Your Bible is upside down, Madam," Tewuh said grinning.

"Wusai palava dei[64]? she retorted.

"We don't even have fufu-corn to eat, much less bread!" the driver said, laughing loudly.

The heated exchange of words came to a stop when the driver suddenly swerved in a desperate attempt to avoid one of the knee-deep potholes on the Tisong-Garinsabo road. Like all the roads nationwide this road had fallen into disrepair on account of neglect.

"When are these coco-yam headed politicians ever going to think of tarring this road?" the driver fumed. He had managed to bring the vehicle back on track.

"My brother, tarring roads is the least of their concerns. What matters to them is lining their pockets and throwing champagne parties every now and then. They are good at belly politics," said a young lady who had not said a word since the vehicle took off from Ndobo.

"What is belly politics, my sister?" Tewuh asked.

"Bro[65], you must be the only man around who doesn't know what the so-called people's representatives do in Yaoundé," she said.

"We go hia nwang for dem hand! No bi na daso tif tif dem de do?"[66] said a stout man seated to the right of the driver.

"One day, one day, dem go meng daso. All we na grong kaku,"[67] the driver said, wiping sweat from his broad face.

"Dem say goat de dammer na for place wey dem tai yi,"[68] another male passenger said, throwing a lobe of kola nut into his mouth.

"They call themselves the spokesmen of the people, yet all they do is steal from government coffers," Tewuh said.

"That's how they serve us! They serve us by serving themselves," another passenger said furiously.

"Look at our schools. They are like refugee camps," the young lady said.

"Take a look at our hospitals. What do you find there? Empty buildings with not even a bandage! A simple fever can kill you in this country," a tout said from the back of the vehicle.

"The most annoying thing in all this is that, nobody finds the situation bad enough to do something about it," Tewuh said.

"Weti you want mek pipo dem do, ma broda? Na wona go big book. Mek wona write book for da tif pipo dem for Yaoundé,"[69] the preacher said.

"The lady has a point. Why are the intellectuals in this country saying nothing about this state of affairs? I'm a university graduate but cannot find a job with my degree. Is that normal?" Tewuh said sorrowfully.

"You can say that again, brother. Me too, I am a graduate of the University of Dschang but no one would give me a job!" the young lady said angrily.

"I thought I was alone in this whalala,"[70] Tewuh said, looking at the girl.

~ 21 ~

"How long have you been looking for a job?" the girl asked. "I have returned from Yaoundé where I almost got killed at the Ministry of the Public Service," Tewuh said.

"Hmmm, Yaoundé! I have heard a lot about that place. I wouldn't even dare to step my foot there. Tell me what happened to you," she said, supporting her round jaws with her left palm.

Tewuh talked nonstop about the humiliation he had experienced in the hands of arrogant aggressive Francophones in Yaoundé. After listening to his story, the Dschang graduate clapped her hands and exclaimed:

"*Ma mami eeh*! And we call this our country!"[71]

She then introduced herself as Yefon.She started to tell her own woeful tale. She said she was returning home from a humiliating interview in Douala where after asking her in broken English how she had learned of the vacancy, the human resources manager of a company called *Etipacol et Fils* had switched over to French and spoke for a quarter hour without looking at her. She said the man did that simply to humiliate her because he knew she did not understand French. She simply excused herself and left the room, weeping.

"That's the way they treat us in the land of our birth, my sister," Tewuh said.

"And yet, we all fold our arms and let them trample on our God-given rights," said one of the passengers who had not said a word since the discussion started.

"That's the sad thing! We give them the leeway to virtually drag us in the mud," Yefon said, dejectedly.

"What do you expect people to do?" the driver asked.

"How bad will things get before we all rise up in open rebellion against marginalization in this country?" Tewuh asked.

"They have guns to shoot you down if you protest. Do you have guns?" the tout retorted.

"My brothers and sisters, an evil tongue is like a serpent! Remember, the Bible says 'blessed are the poor in spirit for theirs is the kingdom of God'," the evangelist, said, after awakening from her deep slumber when the tout mentioned the word 'gun'.

"Madam, mop no get Sunday. Dis palava no be Bible palava!"[72] said the tout, visibly upset at the irrelevance of the woman's remark.

"Ma broda dem, God yi taim na di best. Mek wona no knack skin. All we na pikin for papa God for heaven,"[73] the evangelist, said again.

~ 22 ~

"Madam, what we're talking about is no joking matter. The political system in this country is driving us insane!" Tewuh said, staring directly into the woman's eyes.

"Mek wona no mind! God yi good!" [74] the evangelist retorted.

"The politicians are milking the country dry. University students can't get jobs. Our roads are death-traps. There's no hope for the youths of this country. And you say we shouldn't mind? Is this lady normal?" Yefong said, looking at her blankly.

"Politicians are God's children too," the evangelist said.

The heated argument between the preacher and the rest of the passengers concerning the fate of Anglophones and the state of the nation came to an abrupt stop when they came to a check-point.

"Prrrrrh! Prrrrrh! *Arrêtez! Arrêtez!*" the pot-bellied gendarme shouted after blowing his whistle. He had run out of the tarpaulin tent in which he had been drinking beer and positioned himself in the middle of the road, holding a bottle of jobajo in his left hand.

"Show me les pièces de ton véhicule chauffeur,"[75] the half-drunken officer said, trying to stand firm as he balanced himself on one leg and then on the other.

"Na dem dis, chef,"[76] the driver said, giving him a folder containing the documents of his car.

"*La carte grise, wosai yi deh? Elle est où?*"[77] the officer said, stroking his abundant moustache.

"Yi deh for inside, chef. Na yi dis,"[78] the driver said, pointing at the document he wanted.

"Ha! Ha! Ha! C'est périmé! Yi laf done finish,"[79] he said, pointing his index finger to the date at the bottom of the document.

"I no hia da fabtaleh tok wey chef tok so, chef,"[80] the driver said.

"I say youa carte crise don périmé!"[81] the officer said.

"PeriMary na which paper no, chef?"[82] the driver asked.

"*I say laf for youa carte grise done finish,*"[83]the officer said, tightening the look on his face.

"Oh hooo! I no be sabi, chef. I go get ala one tomorrow,"[84]the driver said.

"Je comprends but you musi donner me un petit quelque chose just now,"[85] the officer said, going through the folder.

"I no get small ting for tchoko chef now, lef'am I go come back,"[86] the driver said.

"*Quoi! Qu'est-ce que tu me racontes-là?*"[87] the officer fumed.

"Na ma first load dis, chef, I no get someting for gee you. Wait taim wey I ton back,"[88] the driver pleaded.

"*Jamais*! Donnez-moi quelque chose maintenant, sinon wona go tanap for ya sotai nite yi com*e*,"[89] the officer said, dragging a chain of nails across the motorway to prevent the car from continuing. He returned to the tent with the driver's documents under his sweaty armpit and continued to drink his beer. The passengers were getting impatient. Some hauled insults at the driver asking him to behave like all drivers normally do and take them to their various destinations.

"Wona small London pipo, na so wona dei. Soso strong hand! I beg go tchoko da tif chef come take pipo mek we g*o*!"[90] the tout shouted from the back of the vehicle.

"Youa mami pima! Na which oversabi de put mop for ting wey yi no concern yi?"[91] the driver cursed, staring vacantly into the vehicle.

"Na me! Go gif moni for dat mange-mille come tek pipo commot for hia. Man pass you, carry yi kwah!"[92] the tout said again.

After standing at the check-point for close to two hours, the driver decided to give the gendarme officer a bribe. He pulled out a huge bunch of banknotes from this chest pocket, rummaged through them until he got to a 1000 CFA francs note, pulled it out, walked over to the tent and pressed it into the palm of the officer.

"*Merci beaucoup*. Tanki too much,"[93] he said, returning the documents to the driver who came back, jumped into the vehicle and took off. From that moment until they reached Garisabon, there was dead silence.

When Tewuh arrived at the Garisabon motor-park, it was getting dark. He did not know where to find his uncle. He walked up to one of the park layabouts who was eating cooked corn and fried groundnuts.

"Tara, how no? Massa, I de fain ma repe wey yi wok for y*a*,"[94] he said slinging his traveling back on his left shoulder.

"Youa repe na who no, mola?"[95] the idler asked.

"Yi na docta Bunkwe,"[96] Tewuh said.

"Yi de wok na wich kain wok, bro?"[97] the boy asked.

"Na divisional delegate, bro,"[98] Tewuh said.

"Oh, I mimba say I sabi yi. Na Docta Cow, n*o*?"[99] the boy asked.

"Docta cow?"[100] Tewuh asked looking surprised.

"Yes, na so all man for dis town de call youa repe,"[101] the boy said.

"Alright, you sabi place wey yi de nang?"[102]

"Yes, gif me small thing mek I go show yi long for you,"[103] the tout said.

Tewuh put his right hand into the back pocket of his *apaga*[104] trousers, took out a 100 CFA francs coin and dropped it into the palms of the youngster who closed his both hands on it and led the way to the home of Dr Bunkwe. They wove their way through several thatch-roofed houses, greeting several people standing idly along dirt streets until they came to a well-constructed one-storey building painted brown with a white garage.

"Na youa repe yi long dat,"[105] the boy said, pointing at the storey building. He disappeared as soon as he had said this. Tewuh walked up to the house, and knocked on the door and a manly voice answered from within, "I'm coming!" He recognized his uncle's voice and felt relieved. As soon as Dr Bunkwe opened the door and saw his nephew he said:

"Is my brother alive?"

"Yes, papa and mami say I should extend their greetings," Tewuh said, hugging him.

"Good, good. Are they well?" he asked.

"Yes, they are both well."

"Welcome, Tewuh. Come on in," Dr Bunkwe said, leading the way inside.

"How are you doing, uncle?" Tewuh greeted, after sitting on a black leather couch in the sitting room.

"Oh, just fine. I can't complain. And how are you doing, my son?" he asked.

"Pretty well, uncle," Tewuh said.

"Good to see you! I wasn't expecting you," his uncle said.

"Nice to see you again, uncle," Tewuh said.

"I am sorry that the last time I was in the village we did not have time to talk," his uncle said.

"I know. You left before the ceremony was over," Tewuh said.

"That's correct. You see, as a believer, there are certain aspects of our culture that I don't take seriously. That's why I left," he said.

"I understand you perfectly, uncle," Tewuh said.

~ 25 ~

"So what brings you here?" Dr Bunkwe asked, wiping sweat from his flat forehead.

"Job search, uncle," he said.

"Oh, my goodness! You leave the city to come looking for a job in a village?"

"I have tried and failed in Yaoundé and thought I should come see you for help."

"You did well to come to see me for help, but there's nothing for you to do here."

"But you are the divisional delegate here, uncle. I wouldn't mind working even as a messenger in your office."

"No, no! That will not sit well with my superiors in Yaoundé and this may even cause me to lose my job. Do you understand what I'm saying?"

"I am trying to understand."

"They might accuse me of nepotism."

"Uncle, you sound a little strange."

"Why do you say that?"

"Everyone knows that in this country, it's man know man."[106]

"How do you know that?"

"I was in Yaoundé lately searching for a job and a friend told me that."

"He may be right but there are exceptions to the rule. By the way, tell me about your job search in the nation's capital."

Tewuh went into a lengthy discussion of his experiences in Yaoundé. He told his uncle how he had gotten into a fist after being openly provoked by Francophones and had almost lost his life. He said he had resolved never to set foot in that city again and lamented the fact that his hard-earned degree had no use in the country simply because he was unable to communicate in the French language.

"I hear what you are saying, my son, but remember that there are many ways of catching the mouse. You don't have to work in Yaoundé."

"I've realized that, uncle but where do I find a job now?"

"I'm glad you've come to this realization."

"Seeing what you mean does not give me a job, uncle."

Sensing that Tewuh was desperate for a job, Dr Bunkwe decided to do something to facilitate the search. He decided to write a letter of recommendation for him.

"Listen, Tewuh, nothing is lost yet. I'll do my best to help you in your struggle to get a job."

"I sincerely appreciate your help, *small papa*."

"I'll write a letter recommending you to my friend, the Manager of the Nun Valley Rice Company at Ndobo. He should be able to find something for you."

"Thanks so much. You think he'll help?"

"Oh yes! Dr Ovasabi is a good friend of mine. We studied at Oxford together."

"I'm elated, *small papa!*" Tewuh said, a look of contentment on his doll-like face.

"There's nothing to be happy about yet. Let's see what Dr Ovasabi finds for you."

After spending five days with his uncle, and his wife, Juliana with whom he had no children yet, he left for Ndobo.

"Take this and use it in paying your transportation fare back," Dr Bunkwe said, giving him the sum of 30,000 CFA francs.

Having said 'good-bye' to the couple, he went to the motor-park to board a passenger vehicle back home. It was 9:00am when he went into a 14-seater DYNA vehicle bound for Ndobo. The driver was a lanky bororo man who smoked profusely and swore without qualms. They had hardly covered twenty miles when a timber-laden trailer went into a head-collision with their vehicle. In an attempt to evade a vehicle stuck in one of the knee-deep potholes on the motorway, the driver of the trailer had overrun the DYNA car. All the passengers where knocked out of the vehicle into a nearby ravine. There was blood everywhere. People were wailing and groaning, imploring the gods to come to their rescue. Everyone was critically injured, except the bororo driver who used his cell phone to call the ambulance service of the Shoeshana Hospital. Several hours after his call, an ambulance arrived at the scene of the accident, with a few para-medics accompanied by two police officers. After successfully resuscitating six people who were bleeding profusely, the para-medics put everyone in the ambulance and drove them to the hospital.

Eight people were declared dead on arrival, including a two-year-old baby. The dead were taken to the mortuary without any further ado. The rest were taken to the ER (emergency room) where there was bee-hive activity. Nurses dressed in blue scrubs, white masks and protective masks scurried around in their mad rush to save the lives of the accident victims. Tewuh was not terribly wounded but he felt excruciating pain all over his body.

"Are you okay?" a female nurse asked, washing and bandaging his wounds.

"No, no! My throat hurts. My back and fingers as well, he said, half closing his brownish eyes.

"Don't worry, you'll be fine," the nurse said calmly.

"Ai! Ai! My finger hurts badly," Tewuh screamed, withdrawing his left hand from the nurse's hand.

At that moment he realized that his left index finger had been severed from the rest of his hand. It was bleeding abundantly. The nurse calmed him down and continued to bandage his wound. Other patients had sustained worse injuries. Some had had their eyeballs pulled out; others had lost their whole limbs. A pregnant woman had given birth to a stillborn.

It took two months for Tewuh to recover. News had reached his parents at Ndobo and they had paid him several visits at the hospital, bringing him fufu-corn and njama-njama soup. They had also brought him bacheukeuh[107] and mbohneuh.[108] His uncle came from Garisabon to visit him. He was very thankful and expressed his gratitude each time his people came to see him. One day, when Pa Kunta came to visit his son, he was told by Dr Tukov who had been taking care of him to take his son home.

"Pa, your son is well now. You may take him home," the doctor said, smiling and putting his right hand on Tewuh's left shoulder.

"The gods are great! Thank you, Doctor, for the wonderful job you did to save my son's life," Pa Kunta said.

"No problem, Pa. Take your son home, he's in good health," the doctor said, offering his hand.

"May the gods bless your work and keep you alive to save more people," Pa Kunta said, shaking the doctor's hand.

"Go well, Tewuh," the doctor said, shaking his hand.

"Many thanks, doctor. I really appreciate all you did for me," Tewuh said, taking his traveling bag from the hospital custodian.

Tewuh and his father took a 504 peugeot clando[109] to their village. As soon as Tewuh sat down in the car, he started to search feverishly in his traveling bag.

"What are you looking for, son?" he asked.

"Small papa gave a letter of recommendation for a job but I can't find it now," he said, still searching in his bag.

"Maybe you lost it in the accident. Please, search carefully; it may still be there," his father said.

"Oh, here it is!" Tewuh said, taking out a bloodstained white envelope.

He was happy he still had that very important letter after the terrible accident. He was worried about the blood stains on it but told his father it would be best to take the letter as it was to the director of the Nun Valley Rice Company and explain what had happened. Women were returning from distant farms when the two men reached their village. When Nah Mbiah saw her son, she put down the bundle of firewood she was carrying on her head and ran to embrace both of them.

"Welcome, welcome! Are you fully recovered now?" she asked, throwing her emaciated hands over her son's broad shoulders.

"Mami, I am very well and happy to be back home. I almost died," Tewuh said, showing his mother the scars on his body.

"God forbid! He will not allow it to happen. He is an awesome God. Hallelujah!" she said gleefully.

Two days later, there was a sumptuous feast in celebration of Tewuh's narrow escape from death. His mother had cooked three pots of delicious food: waterfufu, eru, bush-beef and mbunga. Her four sisters had come from Nguala, Mbeuhmbong, Mbolo and Messi quarters with basketsful of corn-fufu, kwa-coco and bowls of bitterleaf, cutting-grass and kokobioko soup. Pa Kunta's brothers soon arrived accompanied by their wives and numerous children. The women had prepared many dishes of poff-poff and jolof-rice.Their husbands brought calashes of palm-wine and *mbu*. When everyone had eaten their fill, Pa Kunta stood up, cleared his throat several times, and thanked his relatives for coming to join their mouths with his to praise the gods of Ngombi, Ngoketunjia and Ngombu for saving the life of their son. What was left was the cleansing ceremony. The thing that had happened to Tewuh was not the work of men. The gods must have had a hand in it and needed to be appeased.

Pa Kunta asked his son to stripe himself naked. Hesitantly, Tewuh took off his trousers and shirt. His father went into his inner room and brought back a red loincloth.

"Tie this around your waist and take off your underwear," he said, giving the cloth to his son.

"Do I have to be naked for this to be done?" Tewuh asked.

"Yes, you have to be naked," his father said.

When he was properly undressed for the occasion, his father brought out a clay pot full of luke-warm water diluted with the blood and entrails of a ram slaughtered for the ceremony. Tewuh was sitting on a stool made out of the trunk of a fig-tree and bedecked with cowries and beads. Scooping the water in a calabash bowl, his father poured it over his oblong head, muttering inaudible incantations as he washed his son thoroughly using *kuncha*.[110]

When the bathing was over, Pa Kunta smeared the boy's charcoal black body with *manyanga* oil from head to toe. He then put some wood ash into his left palm and blew it into his son's nostrils and ears. At the end of the ritual, Tewuh was stinking like someone who had accidentally fallen into a pit latrine. He was enjoined to not leave the house until dawn. At daybreak he was to go straight to the lake of Ngombi and bathe himself. On his way back, he was not to look back or speak to anyone until he got home. He would put the fresh leaf of the peace plant between his lips as an indication to passersby that he had just performed the beuhbeungkeuh ritual.

When day broke, Tewuh did as he had been instructed. On his return from the river, his father wrapped him up in a sack cloth made of raffia fiber and took him into a hut that had been prepared for him.

"This is your hut from today. You are now a man and can't share your mother's hut anymore. You'll live here until you're able to build your own house," his father said, anointing him with castor-oil.

"Many thanks, papa," Tewuh said.

The next day Tewuh took a proper bath behind his hut and left for the Nun Valley Rice Company. He had not forgotten to take his uncle's letter of recommendation. At the gate of the company he had no difficulty getting permission from the security guards to see Dr Ovasabi.He was a son of the soil fluent in the vernacular.

"Good morning, sir," Tewuh greeted after having been asked to come in.

"How can I help you?" the tall light-complexioned man asked, without taking his eyes off the pile of files in front of him.

"Sir, I have a letter from Dr Bunkwe for you," Tewuh said, taking out the letter of recommendation from his hand bag.

"Let me see it," he said, stretching out his right hand.

Tewuh extended his right hand to give him the letter but he suddenly withdrew his hand.

"Have you been to the ngambe-house[111] with this letter?" he asked, frowning. It was the sort of frown, remote and enigmatic, that one sees on the grim faces of African masks, composed as much of uneasiness as of apprehension.

"No, sir. I don't visit ngambe-houses. Why do you say so?" Tewuh asked, trying hard to conceal his embarrassment.

"It's blood-stained! Can't you see that?" Dr Ovasabi said sternly.

"I see the blood, Doctor; I was involved in a car accident on my way back from my uncle's home in Garisabon. It was a ghastly accident. That's how this letter got stained."

"I'm glad you survived, give me the letter."

"*Tuurrrrh tuurrruh*! I see you have a degree in plant science," he said, tapping his gold pen on his iroko table.

"That's correct, Doctor."

"Do you have a copy of your curriculum vitae with you?"

"Yes, Doctor. Here it is, sir."

"You have no job experience!"

"No sir, I'm fresh from school."

"Hmmmm, it's going to be difficult to employ a green horn," Dr Ovasabi said, biting his thin lips.

"Sir, I need a job in order to get experience. If I don't work, how do I get work experience?"

"Well, my friend, those are the requirements of the company. We need an experienced person."

"Sir, I promise, I wouldn't disappoint you. I graduated magna cum laude in my class."

"You seem quite determined. Are you sure you'll live up to the expectations of this company?"

"Yes, sir, I promise."

"Well, we only have one vacancy at present."

"And what is that, sir?"

"We need a rice demonstrator. Will you take it?"

"Yes, sir."

"Okay, please fill out this job application form and come back after a week," Dr Ovasabi said, giving him a seven-page pink form.

Tewuh was so desperate for a job that he had answered 'yes' without even inquiring about the job description. When he returned to the company a week later, he was offered the position and that was how he landed his first job twenty-four months after graduation from university.

4

The job of rice demonstrator was no sinecure. Rice farmers came to him for solutions to innumerable problems, many of which were clearly above his capacity. Some farmers needed help in selecting the right brand of seeds to sow; others needed help in preparing their paddy rice for hauling. Some wanted him to help them nurse their seeds for the planting season. During the planting season, the rice field was a beehive. Some were planting; others were digging and leveling their plots. Tewuh was always at the beck and call of farmers. He would run from one end of the field to the other and back again. He was trying his level best to be available when needed by every farmer. A sizeable number of the farmers he supervised were illiterate and spoke only in their indigenous languages. This made communication with them an uphill task. Although he was a native and spoke eight of the thirteen languages spoken in the area, he still couldn't communicate with every farmer, many of whom hailed from distant lands and spoke languages with which he was not familiar.

After working for a month, he decided to convene a meeting with the farmers in order to brief them on some in-house rules. He needed an interpreter but was told that the company's translator-interpreter had traveled to Mbenge with the manager and would be there for two weeks. He decided to go ahead with his meeting, having decided to address the group in Pidgin English, a lingua franca in the area. When the farmers were all seated on benches in the company's conference hall, he coughed twice to clear his throat and addressed them.

"Ma kontry pipo dem, I throway salute."[112]

"We throway salute-oh!"[113] the farmers answered in a chorus.

"Just now, na wan moon wey I done wok wit wuna,"[114] Tewuh continued.

"Da wan na turu tok,"[115] a few voices responded.

"I wan tell wuna say ma hart yi glad plenti forseka de fain fain wok wey wuna de do'am,"[116] Tewuh said.

"We tank you plenti-oh for dat shweet tok wey you tok'am!"[117] some farmers sitting in the front row shouted.

"And for the helep wey you di helep we,"[118] some one added from the rear of the room.

"I daso wan tell wuna say I dey hia na for helep wuna. Mek some man no fia for come see me taim wey some ting de hambock yi.Wuna done hia fain?"[119] Tewuh said.

"Massa, we dong hia fain, fain!"[120] farmers shouted from the left end of the hall.

"Die man no di fia bury grong!"[121] a young disheveled farmer said from the back of the hall.

"I sabi say die man no di fia bury grong; but we no de tok na palava die for hia,"[122]Tewuh said, look sternly in the direction of the farmer that had made the comment.

"Tank you massa, na so san-san boy dem dei,"[123] said an elderly farmer seated in front of Tewuh.

"Palava no dei mami, lef'am so,"[124] Tewuh said.

"Ma office na number 666. Yi dey open for wuna all taim; mek some man no fia for come see me. Wuna ya no?"[125] Tewuh said.

"Yeesss, sah, we dong ya!"[126] they chorused like elementary school children.

"Some man or woman yi get question?"[127] Tewuh asked.

The dead silence that greeted his question left him with no doubt that the farmers had nothing to say. The many hugs and handshakes he received from them gave him the impression that the farmers viewed him in a positive light.

When the manager returned from Mbenge, Tewuh went into his office to debrief him on his initial meeting with the farmers. After listening to him, Dr Ovasabi told him that he was very happy to learn that he had struck the right cord with the farmers.

"This company is the economic life-blood of the people you supervise. We've got to nurse it," the manager said, grinning.

"You're quite right, sir. How would all these people survive without this company?" Tewuh said.

"You're doing a great job, Mr. Tewuh. Keep it up," the manager said, standing up to shake his hand.

"I appreciate your encouraging words, sir," Tewuh said, walking out.

Two months after his meeting with the manager, Tewuh was invited to the general supplies office one morning and given the keys of a brand new Yamaha motor-cycle. He was told to use it in the execution of his official duties only. The bike was a huge relief for Tewuh who used to walk five miles to get to his office. To be on time, he had to get up at 5:00am to bathe and eat breakfast. With this new means of transportation he could get to his office in about half an hour. He was so happy that he went to the manager's office to personally thank him.

"I am always glad to help, Mr. Tewuh," the manager said, wishing him a good day.

When he received his paycheck at the end of that month, he noticed a 15% deduction. Not knowing what all that meant, he went to the accountant to find out what was responsible for the drop in his salary. To his surprise, the accountant told him that motor-cycles given to employees are normally paid for through monthly deductions from their salaries.

"Why did someone not tell me this?"

"That's a question for the manager, sir," the accountant said.

"I will go speak with him," Tewuh said, leaving the office. He walked as if he had ants in his trousers to Dr Ovasabi's office. The manager was welcoming technical advisors who had just arrived from Paris and could not receive him. When he finally met with him, the explanation he received made him even more infuriated. The manager told him that what he had done was the way things were done at the Nun Valley Rice Company. He added that if Tewuh didn't like it he was free to tender his letter of resignation without any further delay. Tewuh was so angry, he almost engaged his tall pot-bellied boss in a fist fight. It was the likelihood of spending the rest of his life in jail that stopped him.

The motor-cycle affair led him to investigate the ways in which company money was being used. At first he did not know how to go about it. On second thoughts, it dawned on him that the company translator-interpreter would be a valuable source of information. After all, was he not the main conduit of information in the company? After a few abortive attempts, Tewuh succeeded in making friends with the thirty-year-old man. Having made a few inquiries, he learnt that the translator-interpreter was an alumnus of SAHECO College in Tisong. That gave him enough courage to go closer to him given that he too was an ex-student of SAHECO.The two men started to go out for drinks. Before long, Tewuh was in possession of the most closely guarded secrets of the company.

He told Tewuh that the manager owned a fleet of trucks bought with company funds but registered in the name of his wife. He also learned that Dr Ovasabi was involved in a timber exportation deal with the French government and was reaping enormous benefits from it. He had a well-furnished account in the BNP Paribas bank in Paris where his wife shopped every weekend.

Another top secret that Tewuh managed to uncover concerned the company's chief of the mechanical workshop who was in the habit of inflating invoices on purchases he made on behalf of the company. With the money he got from these illicit deals he had opened a personal auto workshop in town. It was common knowledge in the company that he constantly diverted spare auto parts from the company's mechanical workshop to his own.

Another scandal that Tewuh stumbled on had to do with the accountant. *Messieur* Atangana as he was popularly known had misappropriated huge sums of money from the company's scholarship fund to sponsor three of his numerous *deuxième bureaux*[128] to study in France. Reports reaching the manager on his embezzlement of company money had simply been ignored because *Monsieur* Atangana's niece was the manager's wife. These revelations made Tewuh so angry that he decided to go public with the information he had garnered. He wrote an article on the gross misappropriation of funds at the Nun Valley Rice Company and sent it to *The Combatant* weekly newspaper. *The Combatant* had gained notoriety in blowing the whistle on cases of mismanagement of funds nationwide. Not long after mailing his article, the weekly carried a front-page caption titled 'Grave-diggers at the Helm of Nation's Parastatals' featuring Tewuh's article in its entirety.

The next day, the manager was sitting on his table, his head buried in a copy of the newspaper. He was reading Tewuh's article. He tapped his left foot on the red carpet on the floor, probably thinking of what to do with the culprit. When he had finished reading the article, he went to his computer and sent an email to all the service heads incriminated in the article, summoning them to an urgent meeting in his office. He made photocopies of the article and distributed them to the four men who had answered his call instantly.

"Gentlemen, there's fire in the house," he said, asking them to read the copies of the article he had given them.

Feverishly, they read Tewuh's article. *Monsieur* Atangana was so crossed that he got up and started to walk around the manager's office in circles. Mr Ngong, the chief of the mechanical workshop kept shaking his afro-styled head as he read the article. The others simply sat transfixed in their seats.

"If you've finished reading, let's talk," the manager said.

He had sent his office messenger to fetch Tewuh. He was greeted by ten pairs of hostile eyes as he walked into the manager's office. After giving him a copy to read, the manager asked him if he recognized the article. He scanned it and said the article was his. Dr Ovasabi, scurry-eyed, asked why he had written the article.

"To correct the mistakes of the past," Tewuh said.

"What mistakes are you talking about?" the manager asked, raising his voice.

"The wrongs done to the poor rice farmers," Tewuh said, without blinking.

"What do farmers have to do with an article that accuses the management of this company of misappropriation of funds?" the manager asked.

"Well, there would be no Nun Valley Rice company without farmers, I believe," Tewuh said.

"So what?" Mr. Ngong cut in.

"So the company should cater for their needs," Tewuh said.

"By doing what?" *Monsieur* Atangana roared.

"By using appropriately the funds they help the company generate," said Tewuh.

"Gentleman, you're barely a year old here. What do you know about the financial management of this company?" the manager asked furiously.

"A lot, sir. I know much about the underhand deals going on here," Tewuh said defiantly.

"Underhand deals! Are you out of your mind? Can you provide evidence for what you've just said?" *Monsieur* Atangana yelled.

"The evidence is in this article," Tewuh said, waving his copy of the article at them.

The interrogation went on nonstop for two hours. The manager and his lieutenants tried to wrench an apology from Tewuh to no avail. He stood his grounds, arguing that company money was being misused. He argued that rather than spend company monies on projects that had nothing to do with the company, the management would do well to spend the monies on improving the lot of farmers. The company stood to gain, he argued, if farmers were happy. Realizing that the discussion was leading them nowhere, the manager decided to put an end to it.

"Mr. Tewuh," he said," in my capacity as the manager of this company I demand a written apology from you within forty-eight hours. Furthermore, I expect you to write a disclaimer to *The Combatant* before the next issue is out. Do you hear me?" the manager ordered.

"There is nothing to disclaim in this article, Tewuh said, without looking at him.

"Hmmmm. You're playing with fire," the manager said, asking him to leave.

As soon as he had stepped out of the office, the manager told his assistants that Tewuh would be fired if he did not comply with the instructions given him. They all agreed with the position taken by the manager but advised him to exercise caution given that the matter was already public knowledge. A week later Tewuh received a warning letter in which the manager made it clear that all his movements were being closely monitored. The letter also stated that his continued employment with the company was contingent upon his strict adherence to the policies of the company, notably the clauses that dealt with the sharing of company information with persons not affiliated with the company.

Tewuh was unperturbed. He went about his duties that day as if nothing had happened. At his second debriefing from which he had decided on the spur of the moment to keep the interpreter away, he informed the farmers about what had happened.

"We dey for youa back tara! Go before daso!"[129] several young farmers shouted in support of Tewuh's fight to stop the misappropriation of company funds.

"We di work for ya like jackass, djintete dem di soso tif we moni,"[130] a young male farmer said, wiping sweat from his scared face.

"Helep we put shame for dem head, ma pikin,"[131] said a haggard-looking woman.

"Dem sabi shame? Dem no sabi shame! Dem fit sell popo dem own mami for*seka* moni,"[132] another man said from the back of the room.

"I tank wuna plenty, ma pipo dem. If wuna hia say I done die mek wuna sabi say na forseka wuna,"[133] Tewuh said, adjourning the meeting.

"God no go gring tara, go before we dey for youa back!"[134] the younger farmers shouted as they filed out of the room.

When Tewuh went to bed that night his mind was on fire. What should he do? Write the disclaimer or stick to his guns? He had no problem writing a letter of apology to the manager but not the disclaimer. What would people who had read his well-researched article think of him? What would the editors of the The Combatant think of him? Would they ever publish anything else written by him? He knew the facts were correct. What would he be disclaiming? He resolved that a disclaimer was out of the question. The next day he walked into the manager's office, gave him his letter of apology and told him that he was not comfortable with writing a disclaimer.

"You're putting your livelihood on the line, Mr. Tewuh,"the manager said, as he closed the door behind him on his way out.

The 'Combatant saga' haunted relations between Tewuh and his supervisors. He was prohibited from holding meetings with the farmers without permission from the manager who had put informants on him. Tewuh was so worried he took to heavy drinking in an attempt to drown his anxieties. Out of fear of incrimination, he avoided using his motor-cycle each time he went to Abakwa for booze. He walked to town. Every now and then he would come back tipsy. One day, he went into an off-license bar where several rice farmers were having their weekly njangi.[135] They welcomed him like a folk hero and placed two crates of beer in front of him.

"Massa Tewuh, dis jobajo na youa own dong pipo gif'am,"[136] the group leader said.

"I tank wuna plenty, ma kontri pipo. Mek God yi mua some,"[137] Tewuh said, uncorking his bottle of beer with his teeth.

"Souler Tara, if yi finish we go mua some,"[138] said a chunky fellow wearing a pair of sagging trousers.

"Tank wuna, ma kombi dem,"[139] Tewuh said, pouring a second bottle of beer into his glass.

He kept drinking beer after beer until midnight. By the time he finished drinking the last bottle it was 2:00am. He was so drunk that he took home a whore twice his age. The two of them were drunk. Supporting each other they walked the four miles that separated Abakwa from Tewuh's home. When they reached home, Tewuh was so tired he went straight to bed without taking off his shoes and clothes and slept like a log of wood until 8:00am. It was a Monday and he was supposed to have been at work by 7:30am.

"Na who dis?"[140] he asked, pulling the blanket away from the prostitute who was still deeply asleep.

"I beg gif ma nchou mek I begin go me nayo nayo,"[141] the woman said, opening her owl-like eyes.

"Nchou for wheti?"[142] Tewuh asked, embarrassed.

"Wheti you mean? I know no nang wit you? I beg, gif ma ndo. Back for dang Moni for hand,"[143]she said, stretching out her right hand.

"Lookot! Just take youa foot commot for dis long molo molo,"[144] Tewuh fumed.

"Barlok! Gif ma moni-oh! If no be so I no di shake foot for dis hose!"[145]the woman insisted.

"Commot for dis long! Na who bring you for ya sef?"[146] Tewuh screamed, angry and ashamed of what he'd done.

"See me dis foolish prabrakara pikin! You di take titi come for youa long wey nchou no dey? Nyanga di sleep Man Trobu di come wake up'am,"[147] the whore said, clapping her hands.

"Akwara ting! Commot for ma house! I knack youa kanda?"[148]Tewuh asked.

"Wheda you knack ma kanda or you no knack'am, di ting na say I nang for youa long, gif ma moni,"[149]she argued.

"Ashawo di tif!"[150] Tewuh shouted.

"Tif you too! See me some die man! You sabi sleep woman sef? Since last night you done touch ma dross?"[151]she screamed angrily.

"But no be you be akwara? Wusai me and ashawo commot? Take'am carry youa barlok commot for ma house,"[152] Tewuh said, throwing a 500 CFA francs bill at her.

"Barlok you too, if na cosh!"[153] she said, diving to catch the money as it flew into the air.

The commotion she had caused brought Tewuh's parents to the scene. The woman had turned her back to leave when they got to Tewuh's hut.

"Go to work. When you come back we shall talk," his father said.

"I am sorry about this, papa," Tewuh said, starting his motor-cycle.

It was 9:00am when Tewuh drove into the company premises. Dr Ovasabi was standing in front of his office, looking at his wrist watch. Tewuh said 'good morning' and walked into his office without looking at him. He had hardly sat down when the manager came in, gave him an envelope, and was about to walk out when Tewuh started to apologize.

"I am sorry for my tardiness, sir," he said.

~ 39 ~

"This is the way company money is misused by employees who can't keep to work schedules," the manager said sarcastically.

"I had a family crisis," Tewuh said.

"I need that in writing," he said walking out of the office, his hands behind his back.

Tewuh opened the envelope and read its contents. It was a second warning letter in which the manager made it clear that he would be fired in the event of a third. When Tewuh returned from work that day he went straight into his father's *ntokeuh* or inner room to let him know what was happening.

"My son, the shoulder will never grow taller than the head," Pa Kunta said.

"I hear you papa," Tewuh said, looking sad.

"The hand that visits the anus too often comes out with excreta," Pa Kunta said.

"That's true papa," Tewuh said.

"What has happened to you at your workplace is the handiwork of people with four eyes, people who don't like us and would be glad to see us vanish from the surface of this earth," Pa Kunta said.

"Papa, I don't know about that. I thought it was only my boss who hates me," Tewuh said.

"No, no!" the old man insisted, "What I can see sitting down, you wouldn't see even if you climbed up a tree."

"You're right, papa," said Tewuh.

"When you have some free time, come let's go see Pa Ntumbi," his father said.

"Who is Pa Ntumbi?"

"He's the ngambe-man who lives in the Meusoh quarter."

"Why do we have to visit him?"

"I want him to look into your job situation and give you something to protect you against your boss."

Tewuh's problems were so overwhelming that he could not turn down his father's proposal. He told his father that he would be free on the following kontri Sunday.[154] And they agreed to visit the witch-doctor.

"I also want to talk to you about what I saw this morning," Pa Kunta said, referring to the altercation his son had had with a whore that morning.

"Papa, I'm sorry about what happened. It's all due to alcohol. I drank a bit too much. I'm so sorry papa," Tewuh apologized.

"Listen, son. A woman is like elephant beef; you eat and eat but it never gets finished," the old man said.

"That's true, papa."

"A man's seeds are precious, you don't plant them in barren soil," Pa Kunta said.

"I'm listening to what you're saying, papa."

"You better listen because the next time you want to listen, I may not be here to talk to you."

"You'll live long, papa."

"No one knows, Nyi alone can tell whether or not a man will live long."

"You're right, papa. Nyi knows everything about us."

"Son, you're a man now. It's time you married a wife and started to have your own children."

"I hear you, papa."

"Go to bed, we'll talk more about this when we return from Pa Ntumbi."

The following week Tewuh and his father visited the soothsayer of Meusoh. They rode on Tewuh's motorcycle. As they drove past, men, women and children fled into the bushes and hid themselves behind tall trees. They had never seen a motorcycle before and feared it was some monstrous being coming to eat them up. The sight of two people sitting on the iron monster struck deep fear into the hearts of the villagers. As they got close to Pa Ntumbi's compound a grong bip[155] crossed their path from the right hand to the left. Pa Kunta interpreted that as a sign that the ngambe-man was at home. Tewuh did not know what to make of it. Pa Ntumbi was in his sanctuary when they arrived.

"I salute your bodies," the old man said, inviting them to sit down on bamboo chairs in his medicine shrine.

Lifting his balding head from his ngambe-pot containing several concoctions, he extended a hairy muscular right hand to greet his visitors. Tewuh could not look into the witchdoctor's hooded eyes as he shook his hand. His father did not utter a word. The paraphernalia that lay in disorder in the medicine house scared them stiff. On the floor lay two empty human skulls, the teeth of a chimpanzee, the hide of a boa constrictor, cowries, camwood, tiny calabashes and the smoked entrails of a baboon. Against the wall stood four elephant tusks.

"What brings the people of Batulah to Meusoh today?" Pa Ntumbi asked, gnashing his uneven teeth.

"Pa Ntumbi, my son is in trouble," Pa Kunta said.

"What's the trouble? the man asked.

"His boss doesn't want to see him," Pa Kunta said.

"Why not? Did you say something that is not true?" the witchdoctor asked.

"No, Pa," Tewuh answered.

"Did you say something that made him lay awake in his bed all night?" the witchdoctor asked, looking straight into the young man's eyes.

"I did not say something but I wrote something," Tewuh said.

Pa Ntumbi kept quiet for a long time, as he stared at the dry bones he had thrown in front his visitors. He smacked his thick lips and sighed.

"You wrote something about your boss and sent it somewhere to be published, is that correct?" the ngambe-man asked, without taking his eyes off the dry bones.

"Yes, that's what I did."

Squatting on the dirt floor, the witchdoctor picked up the dry bones and threw them down in front of Tewuh. Narrowing his eyes, without saying a word, he jumped up as if stung by a bee. He made a few dance steps, muttering incantations. He sat down again, crossed his legs and pulled a clay pot out from under his bamboo bed. He placed it on the hearthstones in the middle of the sanctuary, poured brackish water into it and uttered some more incantations. Then silence fell. It looked as if the old man had gone into a trance. Suddenly, he opened his eyes, scratched his close-cropped hair and beckoned to the two men.

"Come, come here! Come close to the pot," Pa Ntumbi said.

Panic stricken, Tewuh and his father took a couple of wobbling steps toward the pot and looked into it.

"What do you see?"

"I see the image of a man," Tewuh said.

"Take a second look and try to see what he has in his hand," the soothsayer said.

Tewuh took a steady look into the murky water. Suddenly he screamed.

"That's Dr Ovasabi! I can see him!" he shouted, making way for his father to see for himself.

"Can you see what he has in his right hand? Pa Ntumbi asked.

"An axe, it's an axe!" Tewuh exclaimed.

"Yes, with that axe he intends to destroy you!" Pa Ntumbi said.

The soothsayer then explained that Tewuh's boss had been so hurt by the revelations he made to *The Combatant* that he was determined to not only fire him but had gone to withdoctors and fetched magan[156] to kill him. According to the witchdoctor, the information Tewuh had exposed to the public was of such a sensitive nature that Dr Ovasabi feared he would lose his job.

"What can we do to stop him from doing harm to my son? I'm afraid he will kill him," Pa Kunta said, disquieted.

"Fear not! Fear nothing! Ovasabi may run but he'll not hide from Ntumbi," Pa Ntumbi said.

"Please, Pa, do something to protect me," Tewuh pleaded.

"Take this and carry it on you at all times," the witchdoctor said, giving Tewuh an amulet and the horn of a buffalo decorated with cowries and porcupine quills.

"Thank you so much, Pa Ntumbi! What would we do against the evil-hearted without you? May the gods fortify you day and night," said Pa Kunta, putting his son's juju in his *nkwo-meunong*.

After giving the medicine-man a bag of kola nuts, a calabash of palm-oil, and the sum of 5 000 CFA francs, they left for Batulah. Armed with a protective talisman, Tewuh felt relieved. As they journeyed back home, his father started to caution him against actions that may put his life in jeopardy. He stressed the importance of peaceful resolution of conflicts and dwelled on the wisdom that lies behind the adage which says that the man who walks away from a scene of trouble is not a coward. He also impressed on his son the dangers that celibacy harbors.

"Your mother and I have sent our knotted rope to the compound of Chui Ndah," he said to his son.

"What's the knotted rope for?" Tewuh asked.

"That's the way our people ask for the hand of a girl in marriage," the old man said.

"I didn't know that," his son said.

"There's a ripe girl in that compound that I think will suit you as wife, "Pa Kunta said.

"I'll think about it, papa," he said, trying to avoid any commitment.

5

Tewuh continued to lead a promiscuous life despite his promise to get married. He drank as much as he flirted. The only time he did not have a female between his legs was when he was walking. When he was full of alcohol, he would start to sing his favorite love song:

Moon commot, njumba commot,
Moon die, njumba die
Nkwang kanda wuna lookot!
Moon die, njumba die,
Moon commot, njumba commot
Akwara wit ashawo,
Wuna chop moni lef ma head!

One day, however, his mother invited him into her hut, saying she had some important news for him.[157]

"Next week your amariya [158] will arrive," Nah Mbiah announced.

"Nah, what are you talking about?" Tewuh asked, astonished.

"Didn't your father tell you about the girl we found for you?" she asked.

"Papa talked to me about a knotted rope you sent to a certain compound but I didn't say I liked the girl. I haven't even seen her. How can I marry a woman I've not met?" he asked.

"Why not? What matters in a woman are good manners, my son," his mother said.

"I know, Nah, but I don't know the girl you are talking about. I can't marry a girl I don't know," he protested.

"Son, don't you trust your father and me? This is a girl of noble birth. We've made an excellent choice for you!" she insisted.

"Nah, you don't know if this girl is going to make a good wife or not. I need to meet her and study her for some time and then we'll see if we suit each other," Tewuh said.

"You waste time, son. There's nothing to study in this girl. Her mother is an exemplary housewife," Nah Mbiah argued.

"I hear you, Nah but just because her mother is good doesn't mean that she's good,' Tewuh said.

"A lamb will never give birth to a fox, son. Trust me," his mother said.

Realizing that the argument was not leading anywhere, Tewuh took leave of his mother and went to discuss the matter with his father. Pa Kunta had left for his raffia palm bush to tape mimbo[159] when he knocked on his door. Disappointed he left for Abakwa to have a drink.

As he walked into Fon's street, he heard a sound behind him, psssh! psssh! He hated that sound because it was associated with prostitutes. Psssh! Psssh! The sound came again. He refused to turn around. Psssh! Psssh! The sound went off for the third time, this time followed by the noise of fast-moving high-heeled shoes kwaack! kwaack! He took all the time in the world to turn around as if he had a stiff neck.

"Massa, some pipo dem de make like say dem di fry dem shit,"[160] said a mami-wata-looking girl, giggling.

"Titi, na youa eye dis? You dong loss-oh!"[161] Tewuh said, grabbing her by her tiny waist.

"Lef me da njakiri tok. I loss you fain me go reach for wusai?"[162] she asked, placing her soft hands on Tewuh's broad shoulders.

"I fain you but I fit nye you?" Wuna nga dem!"[163] he said.

"Massa, wusai you di lancer de go so?"[164] she asked running her well-manicured fingers through Tewuh's afro-styled hair.

They were standing in the middle of the street behaving like love birds. The first time Tewuh had taken her to bed was after a send-off party organized in honor of a technical assistant who was going back to France. He had danced a 'blues' tune with her on that occasion. After the event that took place on the premises of the Nun Valley Rice Company she had invited him to her apartment and they had made love for four hours.

"Nobi I de fain daso jobajo for drink?"[165]

"You ton ton like mimbo-o!"[166]

"Oh ya, mimbo na ma die."[167]

Hand in hand, Tewuh and Rachel walked into Reconnaissance circuit[168] and sat on cushioned leather chairs. They spent several hours drinking Nobra beer and eating a lot of soya[169] until it was 11:30 pm.They left for Rachel's apartment. They had hardly entered her place when Tewuh started loosening his belt and pulling down his trousers. He helped Rachel take off her bra and tight-fitting pair of American blue jeans. She was wearing a *thong*[170] which presented no difficulty at all for him to remove. Then he was on her pounding and pounding and pounding incessantly.

"Hurt me lover boy!" Rachel groaned under him.

"I don't want to hurt you. I just want to make love, sweetheart,"Tewuh said, digging and digging.

After three hours of wild love-making Tewuh pulled himself away from the girl and fell flat on his back. Had it been a Friday he would have spent the night at her place. But it was a Wednesday and he had to be at work in the morning. He looked at his wrist which read 2:30am. Tewuh jumped his khaki trousers, threw on his X-large polo T-shirt and left the apartment shutting the door behind him. Rachel was deep in sleep and did not realize he had left.

It was pitch dark outside. His hair stood on end as he walked home. The sound of an owl hooting in a tree above his head instilled more fear in him. He remembered hearing his mother tell him and his siblings that the hooting of an owl at night was the harbinger of misfortune. He was scared to death but had no choice but to walk home. He had to cross a thick sugar-cane farm which separated their compound from the town. To chase away his fear, he began to sing a well-known hunters' song:

> *Ho! Ho! Ha! Ha!*
> *Pum! Pum! Pam! Pam!*
> *Arata die, na yi mop kill'am!*
> *Frutambo die, na hunter man kill'am!*
> *Koni man die, koni man bury'am!*
> *Ho! Ho! Ha! Ha!*
> *Pum! Pum! Pam! Pam!*
> *Monkey die, na hunter man kill'am!*
> *Nyamfuka die, na yi mop kill'am!*
> *Die man no di fia bury grong,*
> *Ho! Ho! Ha! Ha!*
> *Pum! Pum! Pam! Pam!*

He sang and whistled as he walked briskly toward their compound. Carried away by the melody of the chant he covered three miles without realizing it. He still had two in front of him. As he approached the sugar-cane farm, he thought he saw some silhouettes in front of him. He fixed his eyes on the spot on the road where the figures appeared to have stood but saw nothing. He continued to walk home convinced it was an optical illusion.

Suddenly, four masked men emerged from the farm and fell on him. They were armed with machetes and knives. It happened so fast he did not know how it happened. The thieves beat and stabbed him several times. He was lying in a pool of his own blood by the roadside when the robbers ran way with his wallet, motorcycle keys and the sum of 160.000 CFA francs he had put in the back pocket of his trousers.

A certain Joe Nayi, a palm-wine taper notorious for his nocturnal trips to the bush stumbled on Tewuh at dawn. At first the taper wanted to turn a blind eye and go his way but on realizing that the victim was the son of the quarter head, he went over to Tewuh, touched his heart and felt his pulse to ascertain that he was still alive. He called Tewuh by his name but he did not respond. Heaving the bleeding body from the ground, he put him on his bicycle and pushed it until he arrived at the Pramtati-Pramtata Hospital at 6:00am. He was smeared with blood. The doctor on duty took Tewuh into the emergency room and started to resuscitate him. Joe Nayi left when Tewuh opened his eyes and spoke. He went straight to Pa Kunta's compound to break the bad news. When the old man learned of what had happened to his son his heart failed and he never recovered.

Tewuh was still recovering in hospital when the Quifon[171] came from the palace to bury his father. He never had the opportunity to wash and smear his father's corpse with ground camwood as required by tradition.Pa Kunta was a nchinjia nwonseh[172] and so had be mourned for seven days. His body couldn't be laid in state for everyone to see. As soon as he passed on, his body was wrapped in a mukunta *bag* made out of raffia fiber smeared with camwood and white clay, and kept in the family house next to his father's grave where the Quifon society had to bury him. When Quifon arrived in the evening of that same day followed by the mankohkeuh, mabu and nkehmeundeung, the relatives of the deceased had constructed a fence with wet palm fronds around the house where he had to be buried. The four widows, including Tewuh's mother were asked to line up by the side of their husband's grave. They were shaking like leaves out of fear. The one that was most loved by her husband would be buried with him. People believed that the deceased would need some one to cook his food and wash his back with kuncha in the land of the ancestors. How could he live in the world beyond all by himself with no woman to satisfy him in bed? The women were white with fear. Who was going to accompany their husband? Who did he

~ 47 ~

love the most? Generally, the deceased man would disclose the name of his favorite wife to his chop-chair or heir on his death-bed but Pa Kunta's demise had been sudden; he had not had the time to confer with his successor.

Faced with this thorny problem Quifon decided to bend tradition. Pa Kunta was going to be buried alone. Some members of the society tried to object to this deviation from the norm on the grounds that the gods would be angry and a calamity might befall the entire village. The Quifon stuck to his guns and the title-holder was interred without a companion. To appease the gods, the Quifon slaughtered several goats and rams and poured libation.

It was also the Quifon's prerogative to anoint the heir. After choosing the best behaved man from the man's twenty-three children, the Quifon, smeared him with camwood and sat him astride on the shoulders of the nkehmeudeung who leaped into the air and executed a series of acrobatic feats with the heir still sitting on his shoulders. Stable on the masquerade's shoulders, the heir swayed from one side to the other, holding in his left hand, his father's tchavoom gun loaded with gunpowder. He clapped his hands three times, whistled and then fired three shots into the air *poom! poom! poom!* That marked the commencement of the celebration proper. Four fierce-looking masks like tigers appeared from the fence and danced toward the nkehmeudeung. Then two big hyena-like jujus also emerged from the fence and walked peacefully toward the masks who were then dancing around the big tam-tam in the middle of the ceremonial ground. A royal page was beating the drum with frenzy.

Soon a swarm of bees came out of the house where Pa Kunta had been buried and stung the masks, causing them to run helter skelter, dancing and stamping their flat feet on the ground. Terrified, the mourners fell on the ground face down. They covered their faces with their hands. When they opened their eyes, the bees and masks were gone, leaving the nkehmeudeung and the heir dancing to a dirge intoned by members of the Seven Cup society.[173]

> *Bee gwee-lo! Bee gwee-lo!*
> *Bee gwee-lo! Bee gwee beuh gwia kuuh!*
> Pran! Pran! Pran! Pan! Pan!
> Beuh geh-lo! Beuh geh neuh woh!
> *Bee gwee* Beuh geh neuh woh!
> Prom!! Pan! Prom!! Pan! Pan!

The elders danced, wriggled their buttocks and performed feats. A man threw a spear into the air and caught it between his teeth. Another thrust a needle into his right eye and drew it out of his anus. One of the elders, a diminutive man, ran into the middle of the dancing circle, fired three fingers of hard-baked gun powder, with three bullets, in his right ear, and produced at his left ear a calabash of water, containing the bullets. A hunter kept a gun floating in the air; between heaven and earth. You absolutely have to see these things! The ceremony continued until darkness fell. Seven days later the Quifon and his retinue packed their paraphernalia and returned to the palace.

Tewuh's recovery was slow. X-rays taken two days after his admission into the hospital showed that he had a fractured wrist and sprained neck. Several deep cuts on his stomach made it hard for him to sleep at night. A week later, he started to have trouble urinating. Each time, he went to urinate it felt as if someone had inserted red hot pepper into this urinary tract. He told the doctor who took a urine sample and discovered that he had contracted gonorrhea.

"Have you slept with a woman lately?" Dr Mbuh asked.

"Yes, doctor," Tewuh answered.

"Are you married?"

"No doctor."

"Who did you sleep with?"

"My girl friend."

"Do you practise safe sex?"

"Some times, Doctor."

"Why not always?"

"I tend to forget when I am under the influence."

"Under the influence of what?"

"Alcohol."

"Do you drink a lot?"

"Quite a bit."

"How many bottles a day?"

"Sometimes twelve."

"Waoh! That's a lot. Do you have a drinking problem?"

"No doctor."

"Well, I'll give you treatment but when you are fully recovered I'll like to see your girlfriend as well."

"Thanks doctor."

That day Tewuh's mother came still wearing the black of bereavement. It was her second visit to the hospital. The 63-year-old woman was so devastated that she looked 80. The first time she came to see her son; she did not tell him of his father's passing out of fear of aggravating his health situation. That day she hesitated, but finally mustered enough courage to tell him.

"Son, let's praise the Lord for saving your life," Nah Mbiah said, wiping tears from her brown eyes.

"Praise God, Nah," Tewuh said, holding his mother's hands.

"Where would we be today without Him?" she continued.

"We'd be all dead, Nah."

"Son, Nyi gives and takes at will."

"That's true Nah. He's Alfa and Omega."

"Son, you're a man. What I'm going to tell you may be too heavy but take it as a man," she said.

"What's it, Nah?" Tewuh asked anxiously.

"Son, when you return home, papa's house will be empty," she said.

"What do you mean? Has papa traveled?"

"Yes, your father has traveled to a land of no return," she said and burst into abundant tears.

Tewuh fell from the bed on which he had been sitting onto his mother who had fallen from her chair onto the cement floor. They both lay on the ground weeping at the top of their voices. The commotion in the room attracted the attention of the nurse on duty who came running.

"What's it? What's the matter?" she asked.

"My father is dead! Dead! Oooh-eh!" Tewuh cried.

"Your father is dead?"

"Yes?"

"Who told you?"

"My mother, oooh-eh! Oooh-eh!"

His mother then told the nurse what had happened.

"I'm very sorry to learn about your loss, Mr Tewuh. Take it easy," the nurse said, holding him by the hand. She managed to get both of them up off the floor and seated.

"Please go home, we'll take care of your son," the nurse said to Nah Mbiah.

That night, Tewuh was haunted by all kinds of ghosts in his dreams. They entered, went out, came back, swirled, whispered, and filled his hospital room with deafening sounds of stamping of feet. They rustled behind his bed, near the ceiling, and broke a lot of things into pieces. He could not get any rest in his sleep full of nightmares. He saw all sorts of grimacing creatures, and walking skeletons making hissing sounds.

Two weeks later he was discharged from the hospital. He had completely recovered from the injuries. His mother came to fetch him. When they arrived at home that afternoon there was renewed mourning. A passerby would have thought that Pa Kunta had just died. His stepmothers came and fell on him, crying in a song:

> One never knows the value
> Of a father; a father
> Until he finds the father's hut empty!
> One never appreciates a father
> A father; a father
> Until he finds the father's room empty!
> One never treasures the advice
> Of a father; a father
> Until he finds the father's mouth closed!

When Tewuh had cried enough with his mothers and siblings, his mother asked him to do the traditional thing. He went into the hen-house, caught a spotless white rooster and wrung its neck with his bare hands. He twisted the bird's neck several times until it separated from its body. He collected the spilling blood into a calabash and walked into the small thatch-roofed house where his father had been buried. He knelt down, lifted the small stone that Quifon had placed over a hole that had been dug on the grave at the point where Pa Kunta's head laid and poured the blood into it saying:

> Father, hear my voice,
> The voice of a son who loved you so much,
> Father, here I am standing alone,
> In this wide world without you,
> With no one to advise me,
> Father, I know your ears are filled with earth,
> And you hear me,
> Hear the cry of your son, Tewuh
> Father I know your eyes are closed
> And I know you see me
> watch over your son,
> Day and night,
> In the dry season and in the raining season,
> Be my mouthpiece in the

Land of the ancestors,
Good bye, papa.

By the time he finished pouring the last drop of blood he was blind with tears. He pinched some earth from the grave, mixed it with the blood and made a cross sign on his forehead, chest and stomach. He replaced the stone and came out. That night he slept soundly—no ghosts, no nightmares, and no strange noises.

The next day he rose early, took his bath and walked to his motorcycle. He was going to start it when he remembered that his keys had gone with his wallet and money. In a sullen mood, he walked to his office. As soon as he arrived, he went to the manager's office to discuss the loss of his keys.

"Mr. Tewuh, I'm sorry to hear about your loss," the manager said.

"Thanks for your sympathy, sir," he said.

"While you were away, a letter came from the ministry in Yaoundé, asking me lay off a number of employees," the manager said.

"I see,"Tewuh said, sensing serious trouble.

"And I am sorry to let you know that you're one of the people that have been retrenched," Dr Ovasabi said, without blinking.

"Why me, sir?" Tewuh asked, throwing both his hands up near his shoulders.

"We no longer need your services,"he said.

"Wehe! Na which kain barlok dis eh?"[174] he exclaimed.

"Here is your letter of termination, Mr. Tewuh," the manager said, giving him a white envelope with the company seal on it and trying to conceal a small smirk.

Tewuh opened the letter and read its contents. He was being laid off because the company had discovered that it was illegal to employ someone with a bachelor's degree in a position meant for someone with a General Certificate of Education (GCE Ordinary Level) certificate. Tewuh's plea to the manager to keep him even if it meant he was being underemployed fell on deaf ears. Dr Ovasabi had made up his mind and he had to go. Since he had no motorcycle keys to return, his severance pay would be withheld until he could find the keys.

"I wish you well in your future job search, Mr.Tewuh. Remember, my doors are wide open. Do not hesitate to contact me if you ever needed a letter of recommendation," the manager said.

Tewuh left the manager's office more dead than alive. He walked to the gate feeling like a businessman who had just lost his entire hard-earned capital in gambling. He could not make head or tail of what was going on. He revisited all the misfortunes that had occurred to him in close succession. What had he done to deserve all that? Was it the handiwork of the devil? Was it nemesis? He was talking to himself. His mind was in a quandary. Slowly he walked home, both hands in his pockets. When he got home, he went straight to see his mother.

"Let's go and see Fada Tumi," Nah Mbiah said, after listening to the bad news.

"What for?" Tewuh asked.

"My son, don't lose your temper. Let's go and see the man of God. He will pray for a solution. We can't handle this by ourselves," she insisted.

"Alright, Nah. I don't know what Father Tumi is going to do but, let's go anyway," he said, adding that he was at the end of his tether.

The priest was in the sacristy when the two visitors arrived.

"Hello! Welcome!" Father Tumi said, rushing out to greet his parishioners.

"Good afternoon Fada," Nah Mbiah said, stretching her hand to greet the reverend.

"Good afternoon, mama. How are you doing?"

"Not so good, Fada, the old woman said.

"Not so good?"

"No, Fada," Nah Mbiah said.

"What is the matter?"

"Fada, my son has a lot of problems," she said.

"Let's go inside the chapel," the priest said, swinging his long arms in front of them.

They were sitting in the front pew facing the confessional.

Father Tumi asked Tewuh to tell him what was going on. Tewuh talked to him at length about the accidents he had been involved in, the death of his father and the loss of his job. He was in tears when he came to the end of his narration. Father Tumi heaved a huge sigh and held Tewuh in his hands.

"How often do you pray?" he asked.

"Not often,"Tewuh said.

"Be honest with me. How many times do you pray in a week?"

"Two times."

~ 53 ~

"Why don't you pray more often?"

"I find it hard to concentrate in my prayers."

"What distracts you?"

"Nothing in particular."

"Fada, I feel that the devil is trying to build a home in my son," Nah Mbiah said.

"That may be true. Let's pray," the priest said.

He placed his hairy hands on the Tewuh's head and asked his mother do likewise. Closing his eyes he prayed:

In the name of Jesus,
I command you to depart now!
Liberate his body right now!
In the of Christ,
I order you to leave his soul now!
Free him now!
In the of Jesus Christ,
I challenge you to show me your powers!
Unchain him now! Break the manacles!
Right now! Right now! Right now!
For the sake of Jesus Christ our Savior!
Praise God! Praise our awesome God!
Praise Him! Praise our Almighty God!
Amen! Amen! Amen!

Father Tumi was sweating profusely when the prayer was over. He sprinkled holy water over the young man and his mother. He counseled Tewuh, urging him to steer clear of sinful and unholy acts. He enjoined him to make prayer part of his daily routine. He asked him to pray in the name of the Father, of the Son and of the Holy Ghost.

"Pray to your Father who art in heaven in times of happiness and in times of sorrow. You cannot be too busy to pray," he said.

"Thanks, Father," Tewuh said.

"God listens to his children," the reverend said.

"Thanks for your prayers, Father," Tewuh repeated.

"God well mama," the priest said, shaking Nah Mbiah's hand.

"Many thanks, Fada," she said.

When they arrived home, Tewuh told his mother that he felt a lot better.

6

Tewuh needed a job. He decided to sell his motorcycle to make some money for his job search. A local mechanic who owned a motorcycle repairs shop in Abakwa opted to buy the bike dead cheap given that the keys were missing. Tewuh ran into Rachel as soon as he emerged from the shop, pocketing the sum of 180,000 CFA francs.

"Cheh! You scarce sotai pass piss for pussy!"[175] Rachel said.

"Long time no see," Tewuh said, nonchalantly, his hands in his pockets.

Rachel tried to embrace him but he evaded her.

"What are you up to, baby?" she said.

"Looking for a job," Tewuh said, trying to maintain a calm countenance.

"What happened to your job at the Company?" she asked.

"I lost it."

"What do you mean?"

"They fired me."

"Are you joking?"

"I'm serious."

"What happened?"

"It's a long story. We'll talk later. I got to go."

"Okay, honey. Drop by when you have a chance, okay?"

"Got ya," Tewuh said, turning his back to leave.

Rachel held him by the wrist and whispered into his ear.

"Honey maybe you should try your hand at teaching."

"I never thought of it."

"I heard that Saint Cassava High School is hiring science teachers."

"I'll think about it. Thanks for the info."

As he walked home that early afternoon, the idea of becoming a teacher appealed to him. He recalled the two years he had spent in high school tutoring junior students. He had enjoyed it. He had also been a tutor in his sophomore year in college and had done a great job. He slept on the idea.

The following day he went to Saint Cassava High School to look for a job. Situated on Gainako hill on the outskirts of the village of Vengo, the school was a hub of dropouts from other schools. Tewuh walked into the office of the principal and asked the secretary if he could talk with the principal.

"Is he expecting you, sir?" the lanky bororo girl asked, looking at Tewuh in the face.

"No, madam."

"What business do you have to discuss with him, sir?" asked the girl.

"It's personal."

"Okay-o!" she said, entering the principal's office.

"A little later she came out and ushered Tewuh in.

"Hello! I'm Lewontu, said the principal, stretching his right hand.

"And I am Tewuh."

"Nice to meet you, how may I help you?" Mr. Lewontu asked.

"I'm interested in teaching here."

"Do you have a teaching qualification?"

"No, I don't."

"Have you taught before?"

"Not as a professional."

"Where and what did you teach?"

"I tutored natural sciences in high school and college."

"Great! We need teachers."

"Which of the natural sciences can you teach?"

"Biology, chemistry and physics."

"Wonderful! We need people like you."

"Do you have a CV?"

"Yes, I do."

"Give it to me."

"Here, sir."

"Thanks."

After going through Tewuh's curriculum vitae, Mr. Lewontu asked him if he had copies of his college transcripts. Tewuh had forgotten to bring them. The principal asked him to bring them the following day with a cover letter.

"Our students need a lot of help with the natural sciences. We'll be happy to bring you on board," the principal said.

"I'll be glad to help," Tewuh said.

Two weeks following that interview, he received a letter of appointment. He had been employed to teach biology and chemistry. Those had been his best subjects in college, so he was happy. Since he had never taught before, he was paired with a veteran teacher whose duty was to teach him the ropes. During the first week, he was very nervous. Each night, he stood in front of his mirror simulating a lesson he was going to teach the next day. Several times it helped him out; but often it did not, because class situations are unpredictable. As time went on he became better at the job. Students who were on the verge of dropping biology and chemistry before he came, came up to him and thanked him for helping them stick with the natural sciences.

By mid-semester, the principal called him to his office and told him that he had decided to make him discipline master of the school. Mr. Lewontu said he had taken that decision after closely observing his relationship with the students. Although Tewuh did not fathom that disciplining 1300 girl students was an easy task, he accepted the offer.

One day while he was doing the rounds during recess, he came to the door of a classroom where he heard some strange noises. The door was ajar. He pushed it open and went in. What he saw stunned him. A girl was sitting on the lap of a teacher half-naked. As soon as Tewuh walked in, the deviant teacher stood up buttoning his trousers.

"What's your name?" Tewuh asked the student.

"Vanessa Ngong," she said.

"Aren't you supposed to be on recreation outside?"

"Yes, sir, but Mr. Tamajong asked me to come see him."

"Leave now!" Tewuh shouted.

As soon as the student was out of sight, Tewuh pulled a chair and sat on it facing Tamajong. For three minutes, the two men stared at each other without saying a word.

"What were you doing with that girl?" Tewuh asked.

"Explaining an assignment to her," Tamajong said.

"Oh, come on! Be real! We don't explain assignments to students by sitting them on our laps. Are you a baby-sitter?" Tewuh asked sternly.

"Look, I want to marry that girl," Tamajong said, trying to laugh.

"That's not the point," Tewuh said.

"What's the point?" Tamajong asked.

"The point is that Vanessa is your student. What I saw a while ago is tantamount to sexual harassment," Tewuh said.

"Massa, na we we no? How we go fit fix de palava?"[176] Tamajong asked, trying to strike a deal.

~ 57 ~

"Listen, I'm not interested in stuff like that. We're supposed to be role-models to these students," Tewuh said, walking out of the classroom.

The Tamjong-Vanessa affair served as an eye-opener to Tewuh who decided to probe into the teacher-student relations in the school. What he uncovered was shocking. He learned that Saint Cassava High School was a disguised 'brothel' where students traded sex for good grades. Some teachers had even gone to the extent of housing students in their homes. Many students had been impregnated by teachers who had made arrangements for illegal abortions. Three girls had died in the hands of charlatans. He also learned that two years before his arrival, a senior student had walked into the staffroom, taken off her high-heeled shoe and hit the sharp-pointed end on the head of the French language teacher drawing blood because he had been making love with her and her best friend at the same time. There had been pandemonium in the school followed by a simulacrum of disciplinary hearing and that had been the end of the story. The same teacher popularly known in school and in town as 'banga man'on account of his addiction to marijuana, had been found kicking a colleague on the buttocks in the course of an altercation over a female student they were both befriending.

Tewuh was both overwhelmed and flabbergasted. Armed with a well-written report he decided to take the matter up with the vice principal. He had no esteem for the round-bellied fifty-five-year-old mulato because of his fake mannerisms and haughtiness. Tewuh had once described him to his peers as the personification of pretenses and false values. What he hated the most about him was his speech affectation. He spoke through his nose as if he were a *nansara*[177]. It was rumored around that he was the son of a graffi[178] woman who had befriended a German who worked in the Fort in Buea. Tewuh had to meet with him because he was in charge of student and staff affairs.

Keeping a stiff upper lip, he walked into his office and sat down.

"Whaaat cennn I do forrrr you, Mr. Tewuh?"he asked, taking a wooden pipe from his fish-like mouth.

"Here is a report on some incidents that have happened here lately," Tewuh said, giving him a folder.

For ten minutes, Mr. Ndimassa read the report, tapping his right foot on the cement floor. When he had finshed he interjected.

"Wheew!" This is teerrrible!" he said opening his bluish eyes wide.

"Arrre you surrre about the accurrracy of this reporrrrt?"

"Pretty sure, sir. This is what I found," Tewuh said.

"Come herrre. Let's go to the principal," he said, leading the way.

For there hours, the three men went through every item in the report, making sure there was logic in what Tewuh had written.

"Gentlemen, I can't believe this has been happening under our very noses," Mr. Lewontu said, tears in his eyes.

"Mr. Tewuh, thank you very much for a job well done," the principal said, dismissing him. As soon as he was gone, the vice principal asked what should be done. The principal was of the opinion that the delinquent teachers should be fired without delay. His assistant said he would rather give them a chance to mend their ways.

"How do you allow people like these to teach teenagers?" Mr. Lewontu asked his eyes wider than the assistant had ever seen them.

"I see yourrr poooint, but I'm afrrraid that firrring them may expooose the scandal to the public," Mr. Ndimassa said.

"What do you mean?" Mr. Lewontu asked.

"I think that they may play the innocent by trrrying to tell a differrrent storrry." Mr. Ndimasa said.

"Well, if that happens the culprits will face legal action," the principal said.

"Oookay, I've no objection."

Two days later, Tamajong, Batanga, the 'banga man', and three other teachers were summoned to the principal's office and served with dismissal letters. They were asked to clean their desks and return their keys and books to the secretary before leaving. They all fell on the ground in front of the principal begging for forgiveness. Tamajong cried like a young bride who had lost her husband in a motor accident. He said he was going to commit suicide. Batanga said he was going to commit manslaughter. In the small town of Ndobo where everyone knew everybody, news about the firings at Saint Cassava High School soon became the talk of the town. The aggrieved teachers were so angry that they swore they were going to assassinate Tewuh. He was so scared that he sought police protection but it did not help. The teachers continued to send threatening letters to his home. In one such letter, he was asked to leave the town if he did not want to be murdered. He could not take it any more. He took the letter and showed it to the principal. To his surprise, the principal suggested that he leave the town.

"Where do you want me to go? I was born here. This is my home town," he said.

"I know but the proprietor and I have decided to send you to school," the principal said.

"Which school?" he asked.

"*Ecole Anormale Supérieure* (E.A.S).We feel you'll better serve the students with a teaching diploma," he said.

"You think so?"

"Yes, when you graduate, we'll make you a permanent full-time instructor here."

"I am excited; I like the idea."

"Hopefully, your absence will calm things down."

"I hope so."

"You'll have to go to Ednouay and find your own admission and we'll pay your tuition."

"That's fine. Will I be on study leave with full pay?"

"Absolutely!"

It was a Friday. Tewuh spent the weekend making arrangements to travel to Ednouay to seek admission into E.A.S. When he told his friends he was planning to go to *Ecole Anormale Supérieure,* they simply laughed and asked him if he had saved enough money to buy his way into the school. They said E.A.S was a school where only the children of political big shots got admitted without bribes. A colleague at Saint Cassava told him that her younger sister had given a bribe of 500,000 CFA francs and two goats but still failed the entrance examination because she had not consented to having sex with the director. She said what mattered was not how much you know but who you know.

Tewuh was unfazed by the harrowing stories. He was determined to go to E.A.S. When he arrived in Ednouay that hot Monday afternoon, he was not quite sure what to expect.

One thing he was sure about was that he was not going to give anyone a bribe. To him, bribery and corruption were evils that needed to be eradicated by all means necessary. As he climbed the stairs to the admissions office, he kept repeating the sentence with which he had concluded his article to *The Combatant*: ALL IT TAKES FOR EVIL TO THRIVE IN OUR WORLD IS FOR GOOD PEOPLE TO TURN A BLIND EYE. Strong in his conviction, he walked into the office and greeted a coquettish middle-aged woman sitting behind a stack of files.

"How may I help you, sir?" she said.

"I'm here for admission, madam," Tewuh said.

"Have you completed an application form for us before?" she asked, running her long artificial nails through her abundant dark hair. Her gray leather high-heeled shoes stood by the cabinet next to her table. She had felt uncomfortable in them and had replaced them with a pair of sans-con bata[179] slippers.

"No, madam. I've never been here before." Tewuh said.

"Here you go," she said, giving Tewuh an eight-page blue form. He spent thirty minutes filling it out. When he finished, the secretary led him into the director's office.

"Here's an applicant, sir," she said, giving the gray-haired man Tewuh's form.

"Thanks, Jovita," he said.

"I'm Dr Nformuluh, please have a seat," he said.

"Thanks, sir."

"So you are interested in our school?"

"Yes, sir."

"Good! A trained teacher is an asset."

"That's why I'm here, sir."

"Teaching is like any other trade; you need skills to do it well."

"That's correct, sir."

"So, what did you bring?"

"I brought my Bachelor's degree in plant science and my transcripts."

The question came as no surprise to Tewuh, but the way the man asked it made him think of the comment one of his colleagues had made, describing the director as a compulsive bribe-taker.

"Hmmmm, you're not speaking."

"I don't quite get it, sir."

"You see, competition for admission into E.A.S is cut-throat so you've got to do something in order to have an edge over the others.

"I see, but I graduated magma *cum laude*. I thought that was an edge."

"I know but it's always a wise thing to bring a little kola nut for the selection committee."

"Oh, getting kola nuts is not a problem. Let me go and buy some at the junction," Tewuh said, feigning ignorance.

"It's unfortunate that we're talking at cross purposes. Let me be explicit, do you have an envelope for me?" Dr Nformuluh asked.

"You mean an envelope containing money?"

"Now, you're beginning to speak."

"No, I don't. I thought admission into this school was based on merit."

"Ha! Ha! ha!"he laughed.

What ensued was a bitter exchange of words between the director and the prospective candidate. Tewuh told him in no uncertain terms that he was not going to grease the palm of anyone in order to take an entrance examination into a national school funded by tax-payers' money. He said he would be admitted into E.A.S on merit or never. Dr Nformuluh was about to interrupt him but he asked to be given the chance to finish saying what he had to say. He pointed out that competent teachers were necessary for building the nation but if E.A.S. had become one man's property to be toyed around with, then the Minister of Higher Education should hear about it. Smelling a rat, the director tried to calm him down. He told Tewuh not to overreact. Tactfully changing tactics, he said what he was doing was a way of distinguishing serious candidates from those who were not. He told Tewuh that he if he performed well in the entrance exam he would be admitted into the school. He thanked the director and left the office. On his way out Jovita gave him a sheet of paper bearing the date and time of the examination.

As soon as Tewuh was out of sight, the director came out of his office and walked up to his secretary.

"That one is a hard nut to crack," he said.

"What's the matter, boss?"

"He refused to give something," he said.

"Why?"

"He said he was not going to grease anybody's palm."

"Well, then he'll fail."

"Be careful, he's threatening to inform the Ministry about his experience here."

"Hmmm," Jovita said.

"Keep an eye on his file," the director said.

He returned to his wall-to-wall carpeted office and flopped down on a recliner. He looked like a fisherman who had made no catch after spending a whole day on the banks of a river. He fell into a deep sleep and only woke up when Jovita knocked on his door to let him know it was closing time and she was going home.

"See you tomorrow, Jovita," the man said after clearing his throat.

"Have a good evening, sir. Don't think so much about it," she said.

Tewuh boarded an Amour Mezam bus back to his home town. The E.A.S. entrance exam was scheduled to take place in four month's time. He had to return to his job. When he told Mr Lewontu about his experience at Ednouay he burst out laughing. Tewuh was cross because he did not think the ordeal he had gone through was funny. When the principal had laughed his fill, he clapped his thick hands and asked if he had expected to walk straight into E.A.S. He said the school had been transformed into a 'private enterprise' owned by Dr Nformuluh.

"*Ecole Anormale* is now the private property of the director," he said.

"I can see that."

"He does as it pleases him," the principal said, shaking his head.

"I hear what you're saying, sir, but how long shall we fold our arms and give a few people the leeway to hijack state property?"

"I wish I had an answer for you. He's not alone. If you go to ENAM, IRIC or ASTI, the story is the same."

"It's so sad! Why are we so paranoid? No one is prepared to take up the challenge of fighting corruption in this country."

"It's a national epidemic. Nobody is free."

"I see your point. It has become second nature."

"So what are we going to do? Go give him the envelope?"

"That's out of the question. If I pass I'll go to E.A.S. If I don't I will stay here."

"I'm afraid you may never get into E.A.S if you don't give them a bribe."

"So be it."

The conversation went on and on until the principal asked Tewuh to go home and have a good rest. He said he would convince the proprietor to buy Tewuh's way into the school but Tewuh stuck to his guns. He said he was going to do his level best. If he did not pass then that would be his first and last attempt to study at E.A.S.

The day of the examination came. Tewuh took a Tchatcho bus to Edouany. One hundred and forty odd faces had assembled in front of the E.A.S student union building where the exam was going to take place. Shortly after his arrival, a woman emerged from one of the rooms. Tewuh recognized her. It was Jovita. She held a pink sheet of paper in her left hand bearing the names of the candidates. Garbed in a brightly embroidered African outfit that emphasized her elephantine size, she looked like a priestess about to perform a solemn ritual.

"Ladies and gentlemen," she began, "I say good morning to you all."

"Good morning, madam," the candidates answered in a chorus.

"Now, lend me your ears, we're about to start. You'll be examined according to the subjects each of you will be teaching after graduation from E.A.S."

Silence fell on the crowd. Suddenly someone coughed and sneezed nosily. The woman glared at the culprit and calm returned.

"As I was saying before a rascal interrupted me, we are about to begin. We'll examine candidates in groups. Your names have been pasted on the doors of the building. You'll go round, identify your names and stand where you find them. Is that clear?"

"Yeeeessss, madam!" they droned like elementary school children.

"No name shall be called twice. If you don't answer present when your name is called, you're disqualified at once. A word to the wise is sufficient!"

Hardly had she stopped talking than a short stout fellow wearing a pair of baggy trousers shot up his right hand.

"Sorry, madam, I want to be sure I heard you well. What happens if two names look alike?"

"If two persons bear the same name then we'll examine their faces."

"You mean that only their faces will be examined and whatever they write in the test will be regarded as nonsense?"

The crowd went wild with uproarious laughter provoked by the joke. She felt slighted and barked furiously.

"Look here, young man, you're here to take an important examination; probably the most important you'll ever take before you die. If you mess around I'll delete your name from this list and you can go!"

The threat in her voice was strong enough to silence everyone. They all moved quietly to their respective rooms and the examination started. It lasted six hours. Tewuh was tired and hungry when he emerged from the room but he was contented with what he had written. He immediately boarded a Nissan passenger vehicle back home after having been told by Jovita that the results would be published in six weeks. He was anxious as he waited for the results to be announced. He wondered whether or not he would pass. Having refused to give a bribe, he knew he could count only on God. Tewuh resumed teaching still haunted by fear of assassination.

One day as he was walking down Long Street, a female voice called "Tewuh! Tewuh! Hello Honey!" He turned round majestically and saw Rachel.

"Have you heard the news, honey?" she said as she ran toward him holding a copy of *The Herald* newspaper in her hand.

"What news?" Tewuh asked.

"You made it!" she shouted, pointing at Tewuh's name on the front page of the newspaper.

"Did I make it?" Tewuh screamed, snatching the newspaper from his girlfriend's hands.

"You made it, honey! We have to *arroser!*[180]

"It's too good to be true! Yes, let's celebrate!" he said. They walked to a nearby off-license and drank beer until nightfall.

The next day he broke the news to Mr. Lewontu who was overjoyed.

"Sometimes, God listens to the cry of the downtrodden," he said.

"Not sometimes, God always listens," Tewuh said.

He went from classroom to classroom announcing his departure to the students. Many students cried and refused to stay in class the whole day. Others said they were going to follow him wherever he was going. When the dismissal bell rang that day, a throng of students moved toward him. They fell on him, hugged and kissed him. They shed tears copiously.

"We'll miss you Mr. Tewuh!" some students shouted.

"We'll never have a teacher like you, sir!" others shouted.

"I'll miss you all but I'll be back after studies. Study hard and be good girls," he said, turning away to hide his tears.

The following evening, the principal, proprietor, staff, and members of the board of governors of the school threw a send-off party for Tewuh at the Valley Bar. Teachers and Tewuh's family members had prepared tasty traditional dishes like *koki*, *mai-mai*, rice and beans, corn-chaffe, garri and egusi soup, and more. There was an abundance of local and imported drinks. As the night wore down, Mr. Lewontu stood up and welcomed everyone. He thanked them for taking time off their very busy schedules to be present on that occasion.

"It's with mixed feelings that Saint Cassava High School is sending off Mr. Tewuh today. We're sad to let him go because he's been a great asset to our school.His departure will create a visible vacuum in our staff. At the same time, we're glad because he's going in search of more knowledge which is a good thing for our students," the principal said.

The crowd clapped and hit their glasses one against another.

"He'll be coming back armed with the skills needed to prepare our students for the demands of a highly competitive global market," he continued. People clapped again and whistled jubilantly.

"Mr. Tewuh, you've proven to us that we can count on you. We wouldn't let you down. On behalf of the proprietor and board of governors of this school, I wish you success in E.A.S," he concluded and sat down amidst thunderous applause.

The proprietor, Pa Ntumazah, took the floor and extolled the merits of Tewuh. He wished him well in his studies, reminding him that hard work was the only route out of material and mental slavery.

"Put your head on your books and bring back the academic red feather we're all expecting," he said, proposing a toast.

7

Student life at E.A.S was as hectic as teaching at Saint Cassava High school. Tewuh was required to take many courses, including psychology, linguistics, curriculum and instruction, child development, English, French, biology, math, communication and chemistry. At the end of the school year, student elections were in high gear. The current executive had to be replaced by the beginning of the new semester. Tewuh ran for the position of President of the student government. Like in national politics, students campaigned along ethnic lines: the Ngemba for the Ngemba candidate, the Banso for the Banso candidate, the Bami for the Bami candidate and so on and so forth.

Although Tewuh had no students from his tribe at E.A.S., he campaigned aggressively branding himself the 'candidate for change'. Each time he mounted the podium in the cafeteria to address the students; he called upon everyone to steer clear of tribotics and bellytics, reminding them that ethnic politics is antithetical to the welfare of the students. He reiterated that voting for him was tantamount to voting for transparency and accountability in student government.

"We want change at E.A.S.! Power to the students! Down with politics of the stomach! Away with tribalism! Down with nepotism! Away with cronyism!" he shouted.

"Go Tewuh! Go! We can do it!" his supporters screamed.

"Let's prove that we're capable of governing the nation when our turn comes!"

"Yeah! Yeah! Power to the youths! Go Tewuh! We're behind you, Tara!" chorused his campaigners.

Tewuh's contender, Roland Mbarga was the son of the Minister of Territorial Administration in Ednouay. He hated Tewuh's guts, especially his insinuation that he was planning to get involved in national politics. A week before polling day, Mbarga mounted the podium and denounced the antics of graffi underdogs who had the temerity to think that they could govern Nooremac one day.

"Stop hoping against hope! Since when did second-class citizens become leaders?" he shouted.

"Since the day your father deflowered your mother!" an Anglophone supporter of Tewuh retorted.

The pandemonium that followed that insulting comment degenerated into a free-for-all fight. The Beti launched an all-out assault on the graffi, accusing them of fomenting a Francophone-Anglophone divide in E.A.S. Members of the adversary camps shot stones and broken bottles at one another. Heads were broken, eyes pierced and legs sprained. Before news got to Dr Nformuluh, there were already five casualties. It took the intervention of the mbere-khaki[181] and gendarmes to quell down the campus scuffle.

In the course of the investigations carried out in the wake of the campus unrest, school authorities discovered that Mbarga had given members of the students' Electoral Observatory, a watchdog body set up by school authorities to monitor student voting, the sum of 1.5 million CFA francs in a bid to have them rig the ballot in his favor. After receiving the bribe, the election monitors had stuffed ballot boxes with ballot papers bearing Mbarga's name a week before voting day. The culprits were immediately arrested and the campaign suspended until further notice.

When the director gave his green light for the campaign to resume, Tewuh campaigned day and night, sometimes skipping his meals.

"Truth will prevail! Truth and falsehood are strange bedfellows!"he shouted.

"Yeeehooo! Yeeehooo! We hear you comrade!"his supported shouted.

"Booo! Booo!" shouted Mbarga's supporters.

Out of fear of losing his position, Dr Nformulu had allowed Mbarga to stand elections despite the charge of electoral fraud leveled against him. The fact that his father was a government minister instilled fear in the director.

Tewuh was unfazed. He was articulate and confident. He had the unwavering support of the majority of students who sang songs to discourage Mbarga:

Tewuh eeh! Tewuh ooh!
Tewuh the Lion-hearted!
He that plays with Tewuh;
Plays with fire!
H-u-r-u-je! H-u-r-u-je! H-u-r-u-je!!
Tewuh today, Tewuh tomorrow!
H-u-r-u-je!! H-u-r-u-je!! H-u-r-u-je!!
Tewuh the rock! Tewuh the mountain!

Kum-Kum Massa! Oh Kum-Kum!
One time! H-u-r-u-je! Go Tewuh!

They danced around the campus, carrying their hero on their shoulders. Election day came and he had a landslide victory over his opponent. The campus went wild in jubilation. Tewuh's victory over the son of a minister was a sign of better things to come. On a larger scale, his victory was a pointer to the fact that with free and fair elections, anyone could be the president of the nation. The Francophone supporters of Tewuh sang:

Olé! Olé! Olé!
Nous avons gagné! On a gagné!
Oyé! Oyé! Oyé!
Tewuh pour toujours!
Oyé! Oyé! Oyé!
Tewuh notre président!

His Anglophone supporters echoed the same song in English:

Ole! Ole! Ole!
We've won! We've won!
Oye! Oye! Oye!
Tewuh forever!
Oye! Oye! Oye!
Tewuh our president!

In the euphoria, Tewuh fell onto the tarmac from the can-chair on which four hefty male supporters had been carrying him on their shoulders. He hit his nose and mouth on a cement curb and blood oozed. His hands were bruised.

"Oh, my goodness! Are you okay?" sounded the voice of a female student in her mid-twenties. She stooped to clean the blood from Tewuh's nostrils with a white handkerchief. That was how Tewuh met Natasha. He spent two weeks in the hospital. Natasha and several other students paid him regular visits.

When he returned to campus, Natasha became friendlier. She paid him frequent visits in his dormitory room.

"Natasha, I don't know how to thank you for your concern," Tewuh said, holding her soft hands in his.

"We love you Tewuh. Your accident worried us so much," she said.

"Did you say 'we love you' or 'I love you'?" Tewuh asked, wearing a contagious smile on his doll-like face.

"Both," Natasha said, returning his smile.

"Thanks, Natasha! You're sweet!" Tewuh said, patting her hair.

"Tewuh, it's always a pleasure talking with you. I must be leaving now. I've tons of assignments to turn in on Monday. I came to see how you're doing before settling down to work," she said, jumping to her feet.

"I honestly appreciate your kindness. Please, drop by whenever you've got a moment to spare,"Tewuh said, hugging her.

This was the beginning of a relationship that would last long. Natasha paid him visits on weekends. He returned her visits. She lived on campus as well, so it was easy for him to pay her short visits. The duties of Union president were time-consuming. He had to meet with the Board of Regents every fortnight. He also had to brief the director on student affairs every Monday. In addition, he convened meetings with the entire student body every month to provide updates on administrative decisions concerning on the welfare of students.

One evening, as he lay on his bed listening to music from a brand new stereo set he had just acquired, Natasha burst into his room and slumped onto a chair weeping as if she had just lost both her parents in a car accident. Tewuh had never seen her in that state before. She wore no make-up at all and her hair was in a shambles. Before Tewuh could say a word, she started a long tirade against one of the professors.

"You wouldn't believe what that son-of-a-bitch did to me," she said weeping.

"Who are you talking about?" Tewuh asked.

"Professor Ebotte."

"What did he do?"

"He asked me to come see him after class to discuss my English language assignments."

"Ahmm, and then what happened?"

"When...when I went into his office, he... he..." she burst into tears again.

"Don't worry, honey, just tell me what happened," Tewuh said.

"He took out a packet of condoms from his drawer and placed them in front of me," she said.

"Eh hein! And then what?"

"When I asked him what the condoms were for, he said he was to use them," Natasha said.

"Okay, and then what?" Tewuh asked.

"As soon as he said that, he stood up and threw down his trousers and under wear," Natasha said.

"Are you serious?"

"What do I gain from telling a lie?"

"Good! I have been looking for evidence to substantiate the sleazy stories I've been hearing about Dr Ebotte. I now have it!"

"It's a scandal! What does he take me for? A whore or what?"

"Don't worry, my love. I'll get to the bottom of this matter."

Natasha's confrontation with Professor Ebotte served as a stimulus for Tewuh to carry out an investigation into students' relationship with professors at E.A.S. He created opinion boxes which were placed in every classroom, asking students to drop in their comments on their relations with professors. After five days the boxes were full of complaints. Student grievances included examination malpractices, sexual harassment, the trading of influence and verbal abuse. In one of the boxes, Tewuh read a note in which a female student complained that a professor who was chairing her thesis committee had threatened to dissolve the committee if she did not yield to his sexual advances. There were complaints against male professors who were writing theses for the female students they were befriending. The most telling grievances came from Anglophone students who complained about the linguistic apartheid at E.A.S. A student complained bitterly about the haughty attitude of Francophone professors who were notorious for deriding Anglophone students on account of their lack of proficiency in the French language. Tewuh empathized with the students because he had more than once been asked by the Francophone professor to "*parlez correctement le français*".

He convened a meeting of the student Exco and presented the list of grievances to them. For six hours, they went through each complaint, deliberating on the course of action to take. At the end of the meeting, there was a consensus that the first step would be to take the matter up with the Board of Regents. As the president of the Students' Union, Tewuh was a sitting member of that 18-member governing body. He had played a critical role in establishing a workable framework for shared governance at E.A.S.

When the matter was brought to the attention of the student body, it was decided to send a delegation comprising the Union president, vice-president, secretary-general and treasurer to the director of the school. On second thoughts they decided to let

Natasha be part of the delegation, just in case first-hand evidence was needed.

Dr Nformuluh was in his office giving instructions to Jovita on how to handle certain files when the delegation arrived.

"How may I help you ladies and gentlemen?"he asked, looking over the pile of files that sat on his table.

"We have a problem to discuss with you, sir,"Tewuh said.

Dr Nformuluh quickly dismissed his secretary and asked the students to sit down.

"What's the problem?" he asked.

"Here sir," Tewuh said, giving him the petition written by the Exco on the behalf of all the E.A.S students.

He read through the document in ten minutes, threw his head back and asked the students if they had evidence to buttress their allegations. At that time, Natasha stood up and spoke. She told the director what had transpired in Professor Ebotte's office. The pupils of the director's eyes dilated as Natasha elaborated on the details of the professor's lecherous misconduct.

"Thank you for bringing this to my attention. I will look into the matter without delay," the director said, dismissing the students.

"Thank you, sir. We'll be waiting for your feedback," Tewuh said.

One week went by, then two, then three. The student delegation heard nothing from the school authorities. After one month, Tewuh made another appointment to see the director. As soon as he walked into the office, Dr Nformuluh asked him to shut the door behind him.

"Mr. Tewuh," he said, "I have to start by apologizing for the delay in getting back to you."

"No problem, sir. I know you're a busy man."

"I have made my inquiries and found out that there is some truth in the students' complaints."

"Alright, so what's the fate of those professors?"Tewuh asked, looking directly into the man's eyes.

"I'll serve them with warning letters," the director said, scratching his moon-head.[182]

"And that'll be it?" Tewuh asked, an expression of disappointment on his face.

"Yes."

Dr Nformuluh then went into a lengthy explanation. He told Tewuh that to safeguard the image of E.A.S it would be better to not expose the conduct of the delinquent professors to the public. He said donors could use those incidents to stop providing funds to the institution. Worse still, politicians could seize the opportunity to sow seeds of discord on the campus to tarnish the image of E.A.S.

"Sir, the image of this institution is already tarnished. Some of the stories are in the streets already," Tewuh said.

"Who told you that?" the director asked, looking worried.

"The grapevine," Tewuh said.

"Leave the issue to me," the director said, asking Tewuh to leave.

It was a dejected Tewuh that left the director's office that afternoon back to the union cafeteria to attend a scheduled Exco meeting. When he communicated the director's reponse to the executive committee of the Students' Union, there was fury.

"We're not going to take this lying down. The director is condoning evil," the secretary-general said.

"What does he mean by 'sow seeds of discord on the campus'?", the vice-president asked.

"Sweeping the problem under the carpet won't make it go away. It'll only get worse," the treasurer said.

"The fact of the matter is that some professors are abusing their positions, and should be made to stop," Tewuh said.

"So what are we going to do now?" the secretary-general asked.

"I think we should give the students the chance to make a decision," Tewuh said.

The next day, the Exco convened a meeting of the student body in the gymnasium. During the deliberations, speaker after speaker stood up to denounce the unethical comportment of teachers at E.A.S. Many decried the misappropriation of funds by the director. A student claimed that Dr Nformuluh had bank accounts in Switzerland and France well furnished with money collected illegally from prospective students. She added that the director owned real estate and a fleet of taxis in Bamenda, Kumba, Douala and Yaoundé. Another student revealed that Dr Nformuluh had several mistresses studying in the United States of America and Canada on scholarships provided by him. There was an outcry from almost all the students against what they called the privatization of E.A.S. by the director.

"When is the world going to be told that E.A.S is an institution where diplomas are traded for money and sex?" an angry student lamented.

An albino speaking in a shrill voice said the bursar of the school owned *mini-cités*[183] all over the city constructed with money stolen from the school's coffers. A Bassa student told the assembly that the cafeteria boss owned countless shops in town stocked with provisions stolen from the school's storeroom.

When the meeting adjourned at 4:00pm, there was unanimous agreement that the students should embark on a protracted strike until their grievances were addressed. The following morning, Tewuh put up a notice on the bill board at the Union that read:

CALL TO STRIKE!!!
CORRUPTION IS A CANKER THAT'S EATING
DEEP INTO THE FABRIC OF E.A.S. WE MUST ACT
NOW OR PERISH!
BOOKS DOWN! PENS DOWN! OUR CRY MUST BE
HEARD!
DOWN WITH KABU-KABU PROFESSORS!
AWAY WITH KOKOBIOKO TEACHERS!
TO HADES WITH PSEUDO-INTELLECTUALS!
SIGNED: PRESIDENT AND EXCO OF THE E.A.S.
STUDENTS' UNION

The strike started as soon as the notice was posted. Students carrying placards marched peacefully to the administrative building, calling for the director to come out and address them. Panick-stricken, Dr Nformuluh immediately picked up his phone and dialed the office of the superintendent of police and told him that his life was in jeopardy. In less than no time, the campus was flooded with men and women in uniform, carrying guns, tear-gas canisters and batons. The strike that had started as a peaceful demonstration turned into a violent confrontation between the students and forces of law and order. Rampaging students engaged in running battles with armed policemen and soldiers. While the troops fired gunshots into the air, the mob responded with volleys of stones. Then the troops riposted, tossing tear-gas canisters. Unemployed university graduates, bandits and criminals from the streets soon joined the students to express their discontent against those in power for not creating enough employment opportunities for them. Then an orgy of violence, savagery, brutality and looting of public property began.

Several students were shot dead by trigger-happy forces of law and order who continued to fire live bullets at unarmed fleeing demonstrators. The irate students proceeded to the administrative building and set it on fire. The director's office burnt to ashes. The students shouted slogans reiterating that the most soothing words must come from the director himself but he had gone into hiding. A semblance of calm returned to campus after eight hours of incensed violence resulting in the death of fifty-seven students. Dr Nformuluh was nowhere to be found. Later that evening, he appeared on national television and made a vitriolic speech. In less than five minutes he defiantly told the 'demons' instigating riots at E.A.S in order to score political points that their efforts were doomed. He accused the main opposition party in the country of being the brain behind the student unrest. He said those who had failed to win power by the ballot and had turned to the students to destabilize the nation, should hide their faces in shame. As for the students who were being used as pawns on the political chessboard, he said they were going to pay dearly for their deeds.

Shortly after the director's provocative speech, students went amok again, destroying and looting anything they found on their way. They burned and ransacked every car on the campus and in the surrounding streets.

The angry crowd evacuated computers and electronic gadgets, money and other valuable property and burnt them outside the administrative building.

Troops returned to campus with alacrity determined to wreak havoc. They beat and dragged naked students in mud. They frog-marched male students, making them repeat the phrase 'my degree is a piece of shit' several times. Female students were raped by soldiers in broad daylight. Girls who tried to resist rape had beer bottles and cigarette butts inserted into their vaginas.

An inventory conducted by Transparency Without Borders (TWB) indicated that two hundred and ten students lost their lives as a result of the strike. A week later, the French-speaking Minister of Communication Professor Fabrice K. Kontchou was interviewed by a private TV channel, Equinoxes, and asked to comment on the estimated number of casualties at E.A.S. following the student strike. Keeping a straight face, he said 'zéro mort', which could be translated as 'zero dead'. This falsification of facts earned the minister the nickname 'Le Ministre Zéro Mort', which could be translated as 'Minister Zero Dead'.

Tewuh, who had smelled a rat, had escaped to his hometown. When he resurfaced on campus five days later he was led in handcuffs to the Kondengui Maximum Security prison which became his home for six months.

8

It was already the beginning of a new semester when he was released from jail. He had lost an entire semester but was determined more than ever before to obtain his teaching qualification. Natasha wept for joy when she set her eyes on her fiancé. The two threw themselves at each other and kissed endlessly.

"I feared for your life, honey," Natasha said wiping tears from her greenish brown eyes.

"That's the price we pay for being beasts of no nation sweetheart," he said.

When summer vacation came, Tewuh decided to take Natasha to his mother and relatives. She was ill at ease as they walked down Long Street into Batula Quarter. Quite apart from the butter flies that normally flutter in a woman's belly when she has to meet her prospective in-laws for the first time, there was the added fear of the land dispute that had pitted the village of Lohmeukoh against the people of Lohbeujiah, Natasha's native village. She held her heart as they approached the compound. It was early in the morning and Tewuh's mother hadn't left for her farm at Ntango yet. The children in the compound saw them first and started to shout— "welcome!", "welcome!"— as they ran toward the newcomers.

Tewuh's mother came out wiping her wet hands on her wrapper and cleaning woodash from her graying hair. She had been cooking corn-fufu on firewood. She held her son close to her chest. Tewuh towered over his mother and had to bend almost double in order to properly embrace her. His mother then turned to Natasha and said: *"agwe meh"*, which could be translated as "welcome". Natasha did not understand the vernacular greeting. She simply smiled and shook her hand. Tewuh told his mother that Natasha was his friend. The old woman nodded.

At the moment, Tewuh's uncle Pa Taboh came out of the house that had previously been inhabited by Tewuh's father. Tewuh left Natasha and his mother and moved toward him. He embraced him and shook hands with him. Pa Taboh turned and looked at Natasha and said to Tewuh: *"Be viya no meh?"*, which could be translated as: "Is this your wife?" He was only teasing because according to tradition, it was his duty to look for a wife for his nephew.Tewuh smiled broadly and said nothing. He did not want to let the cat out of the bag too soon. He went with this uncle into the house; a house Pa Taboh had inherited together with Tewuh's mother and three co-wives.

Natasha followed Tewuh's mother into the kitchen. They were there for a while then Tewuh came out and went over to meet the women. Natasha looked into his face trying to figure out what he had been discussing with his uncle. Before he came Tewuh's mother had been asking her about their journey. It was her way of being courteous because there was not much they could talk about at length given the language barrier that separated them. In her attempt to communicate in Pidgin English, Tewuh's mother made some blunders. For example, in an attempt to ask Natasha if she had slept well, she said "you shit fine?" in stead of" "You sleep fine?" In a similar vein, in trying to say that the distance between the city and the village is long she said: "Na long load", instead of "Na long road". She soon excused herself and continued with her cooking.

She looked at her son from time to time as she went about her chores. She was probably wondering what Natasha meant to him. After having eaten a delicious meal of corn-fufu and vabeuteh[184], Tewuh led Natasha to his uncle's house where he welcomed them as if they had just arrived. Sending his right hand into his kwoh meunong[185], he took out two unpeeled kola-nuts and gave one each to his visitors. He then asked Tewuh to peel his own and drop the peelings on the dirt floor in front of him. Tewuh did as he was told. The old man looked at the five peelings in front of his nephew, squinted and said:

"Some one is going to get married. Who is it?"

Tewuh and Natasha looked at each in surprise.

"I don't know uncle," he said.

"Hmmm, it's right there in front of you. Look at the peelings," he said.

Tewuh took a second look at the kola-nut peelings but deciphered nothing. The old man sent his hairy hand and picked up the peelings, held them up in front of his visitors and said:

"Look here, this is the male and here is the female. They are together."

"I don't understand uncle," Tewuh said.

"One day, you'll understand," he said, bringing out a calabash of palm-wine from under his bamboo bed. After coughing three times, he called: "Dubeuh! Dubeuh!"

"Yeuh!" answered Tewuh's youngest brother.

"Bring us two cups from your mother's kitchen," Pa Taboh said.

He poured palm-wine into his ndeuh mbeuh[186], ran his forefinger over the foams to clean dirt and poured some of the palm-wine on the floor saying: "This is your share, gods of our forefathers." He started to drink. When Dubeuh arrived with the Indian bamboo cups, Pa Taboh poured wine first into Tewuh's cup and then into Natasha's. It was obvious from the man's gestures that he suspected what had brought the two young persons home that day. But it was hard to tell whether or not he was pleased. He maintained a stony countenance throughout their visit. Tewuh's mother soon came in carrying a bowl of fried groundnuts and cooked corn. This was to serve as dessert for the heavy meal they had just eaten. As they ate, Pa Taboh said to his nephew:

"Son, if you own a rooster that never crosses a hen would you call it a rooster?"

"No, uncle," Tewuh answered.

"When you arrived home this morning with this young lady, I did not tie my mouth; I asked you if she was your wife," the old man said, throwing a lobe of kola nut into his mouth.

"That's correct uncle," Tewuh asked.

"The woman who gave you birth is sitting here now. I am going to ask you the question again."

"No problem, uncle."

"Who is this woman to you?"

"She's the woman with whom I'd like to spend the rest of my life."

Silence fell in the room. Pa Taboh looked at Tewuh's mother and she looked at him. Pa Taboh scratched the back of his head thrice, swallowed the kola nut he was chewing and took a sip of his palm-wine.

"Is that so, my son?" the old man asked.

"Yes, uncle," he said.

"Are you serious?"

"Very serious, uncle. I can't live without her. She saved me from death."

Pa Taboh drank again from his cup before responding.

"How did she save your life?" the old man asked.

Tewuh recounted the accident at E.A.S and explained in detail the role Natasha played in his recovery. He said Natasha took care of him just as if she were his mother.

"I'm glad to hear that, son."

He turned to Natasha and thanked her for doing what she did. Tewuh's mother also thanked her. Very pleased, Natasha simply smiled.

"Where do her parents live?" Pa Taboh asked.

"Her parents live in Lohbeuhjia," Tewuh said.

As soon as the word Lohbeuhjia came out of Tewuh's mouth, darkness fell in the room. His uncle looked at his mother who had covered her face with both hands. Pa Taboh kept his head down for about five minutes, staring into the blank in front of him. He kept sighing but said nothing. Tewuh felt very uneasy and asked his parents if something was the matter.

"Son, this is a difficult knot. We can't tie it," the old man said at last.

"Why not?" Tewuh asked anxiously.

"Son, don't you know that our people are at war with the people of Lohbeuhjia?"

"No I didn't know that." Tewuh said, shaking his head.

"Where have you kept your ears, son? The people of Lohbeuhjia are fighting us because of land!"

"They've killed some of our people already. How can you marry their daughter?" Tewuh's mother cut in.

"Does that really matter? The two villages may be at war but Natasha and I are not at war!"Tewuh said, raising his voice.

"Son, how are we going to buy your wife if our people aren't allowed to set foot in the village of Lohbeuhjia?" his uncle asked.

The conversation was becoming inconclusive. Pa Taboh insisted that Tewuh could not marry Natasha because a few farmers from her village had disregarded the line of demarcation drawn by the ex-colonial masters between the two villages and had attacked and killed three farmers from the village of Lohmeukoh, Tewuh's birthplace. Tewuh tried hard to convince his parents that the incident was inconsequential as far as their marriage was concerned. At that point he asked Natasha, who had been mute, to say something about the remarks his parents had just made.

In a soft voice, she told Tewuh's parents that at first her parents did not want to hear about her marriage to a man from Lohmeukoh. However, they had given their blessing after she told them that the skirmishes between their two villages were likely to come to an end once sons and daughters from both sides started to inter-marry. She said she had pointed out to her parents that nobody would be foolish enough to declare war against his in-laws. Tewuh's mother and uncle kept nodding their heads as she spoke.

When Tewuh and Natasha left for E.A.S the following day, arrangements had been made for the knack door.[187] Before they left the compound, he had agreed with his uncle that a delegation of family members would pay a courtesy visit to the family of Natasha in order to inform them of their intention to steal a chicken from their compound. The delegates were chosen with great care. Pa Taboh was designated as the leader and spokesperson of the group. Tewuh had given him enough money to buy drinks and some bottles of Majunga and Johny Walker whisky. [188] An impressive entourage of young women from the family circle accompanied Tewuh's mother and carried firewood and food items. She carried a piece of cloth, a basket full of kola nuts, and some tobacco and snuff meant for the bride's mother and father who had been informed about the visit. They were waiting.

It was the market day in the village of Lohbeuhjia. The delegation arrived at 9:30am and was led to the compound of Natasha's parents by a teenager who had been asked to wait at the Three-Corner motor park. The visitors were taken to the father's house and shown seats. They stole glances at the spacious living room filled with modern appliances: TV set, DVD player, boom box and refrigerator. Some high-life music was playing in the background. They were happy because the nature of a man's residence said a lot about his mindset. The building had eight rooms, including an internal kitchen. Natasha's father was a businessman who owned a fleet of taxis and bendskin plying the Lohbeuhjia-Lohmeukoh road. He had made a lot of money from his trade in gunpowder which he had used to build the storey-building in which his visitors where sitting. This show of wealth gave the visitors the assurance that their son was not getting married to a girl from a wretched family who would shift their responsibilities to them.

After about a quarter hour, Natasha's father drove into his compound in an SUV, jumped down and threw his impeccably white agbada[189] over his broad shoulders before going into the house. His visitors all stood up when he walked in. His well polished black *Pierre Cardin* shoes clacked on the cement floor as he walked.

"Welcome, welcome, please sit down," he said, smiling and shaking everybody's hands.

His wife came in on his heels dressed gorgeously in an embroidered boubou[190] made in Cotonou.She greeted everyone and left the room instantly. The knack-door was essentially a men's affair where women were often kept out even though it was about their fate, their future.

Having chatted with his guests for a couple of minutes, Natasha's father asked for permission and stepped out.

"Musa! Musa!" he called.

There was no answer. As he raised his voice to call loudly, a boy in his teens emerged from the bushes.

"I'm here, papa."

"Where were you? Didn't I tell you to be around to run errands for me?"

"I was not far, papa," the boy said, gasping for breath.

"You weren't far but couldn't hear me? Go and tell Pa Jamai to come," he whispered to the boy.

The boy ran to his uncle's compound and returned. Pa Jamai soon appeared. Other relatives who had been invited began to pour into the compound. When Pa Jamai arrived, his younger brother invited him to come over and sit close to him. The visitors were seated on the East wing of the house facing Natasha's relatives. When the room was filled with people, Natasha's father stood up, cleared his throat and spoke.

"Brothers and sisters, on behalf of my family I want to welcome you all to this compound," he said, beaming at his visitors.

"Thank you, Pa! We're very glad to be here today," the visitors chorused as if they had rehearsed their response.

"These people are from Lohmeukoh," he said, "when I heard they're coming, I said I couldn't receive them alone."

"You did well. Those who live alone, die alone!" Pa Jamai said.

"Thank you everyone for being here today. Our visitors are here. Our ears are open, let them tell us what brought them to this compound," he said, sitting down.

Pa Taboh stood up, cleared his throat twice and began to speak. The old man had the gift of the gab.

"On behalf of my brothers and sisters from Lohmeukoh, I say many thanks to the father of this compound who has thrown his doors open to us."

"Thank you for coming," said Natasha's father.

"Our people say that the height of a man is measured by the string of well-wishers he has," Pa Taboh continued.

"You couldn't have said it better," Pa Jamai said.

"The purpose of our visit is certainly no secret to you but let me start by introducing members of my family here present."

He proceeded to introduce every member of his entourage, saying how they were related to him. Then he continued.

"We're here today because we're chicken thieves."

"Hmmmm! Hmmmm!" the hosts groaned.

"We've seen a pretty chicken in this compound that we'd love to steal," he said and kept quiet.

There was protracted silence that was broken by Pa Jamai.

"We've several chickens in this compound but they've all left the roost. If you'd told us earlier, we'd have locked the hen-house," he said.

The crowd burst into laughter. They were enjoying Pa Jamai's play with words.

"You're not getting me. That's not what I meant," Pa Taboh said.

"Well, why then are you speaking as if you'd a calabash full of water in your mouth?" Pa Jamai said.

The crowd went wild with laughter again. Even though moments like these were not meant for jokes, the people could not help laughing at the way Pa Jamai and Pa Taboh avoided the topic at hand while simultaneously approaching it.

"I mean that we've seen a beautiful girl in this compound that suits our son," Pa Taboh continued.

"Did you hear what he said?" Pa Jamai asked, turning to his relatives.

"Yeeeesss, we heard him with our own ears!" they said in unison.

"What do you say about his request?" Pa Jamai asked, looking at his relatives.

He waited for some time for someone to speak but no one opended his mouth. He turned to Natasha's father and said:

"Njinjo, what do you have to tell them?"

"All I have to say is that thieves don't come in broad day light. A daylight thief is a good thief. Let them choose the chicken they want to steal," Pa Njingo said.

Pa Jamai turned to his visitors and asked if they had heard the response of Natasha's father. Pa Taboh said he had heard.

Turning around Pa Jamai saw a female member of the family who had just come in and sat among the men. He went over to her and asked her to go and call Mah Titi, Natasha's mother. As the woman was about to leave, he whispered in her ear, enjoining her to remain in the kitchen with the other women. Soon Mah Titi came into the room and sat behind her husband. He spoke into her ear and she left immediately.

"I have four daughters," Pa Njinjo said, "They'll come in one by one and you can make your choice."

Soon Natasha's youngest sister came in wearing nothing but a string of beads and colorful loincloth. She moved to the center of the room, bowed and clapped her hands thrice in the form of a greeting.

"Is that the one you like?" Pa Njinjo asked.

"No-ooh!" the visitors answered.

The second one came in dressed like the first. She performed the same gesture.

"Is this the girl you want?" Pa Njinjo asked again.

"No-ooh!" the visitors answered again.

The third daughter came in dressed in a loincloth steeped in camwood. She performed the traditional gesture.

"This must be the one you want," Pa Njinjo said.

"No-oooh!" the visitors shouted.

The last daughter came in dressed like the third and did the customary thing.

"Well, this is my last daughter. Is it she?" Pa Njinjo asked.

"No-oooh!" the visitors answered again.

"Too bad! You don't seem to like any of my daughters. I'm sorry you've made a futile trip to my compound," Pa Njinjo said.

"Are these all your daughters? You don't have another daughter who is not here?" Pa Taboh asked.

Pa Njinjo tilted his head to one side and acted as if he were trying to remember something.

"I've got one more daughter but she's not here. I'm sure you've never seen her because she lives in Ednouay," Pa Njinjo said.

"Yeesss, we have seen her! That's the one we want!" the guests screamed.

"That's the woman I want for my son," Pa Taboh said calmly.

"That one? No, no! I can't let her go. She's studying at a big university. When she finishes she'll earn a lot of money for me," Pa Njinjo said.

"We will give you whatever you want. My son will not live without her. Please, pleeasssse! Grant our wish!" Pa Taboh pleaded.

He pointed out that his son was also studying at a big university and that together he and his wife would give Pa Njinjo whatever he wanted.

"Are you telling me that the man who desires my daughter as wife is not even here?" Pa Njinjo asked.

"Children of nowadays are ignorant of tradition. He should have been here but he said he'd urgent business at school," Pa Taboh explained.

Pa Njinjo kept his head down for a few minutes. There was expectant silence in the house. Nobody coughed; not one person talked. There was visible tension on the side of the vistors. They were all wondering what the compound head was going to say.

"Has your son met my daughter?" he asked.

"Yes, in fact, my son and your daughter are in the same university," Pa Taboh said confidently.

"Have you met my daughter?" Pa Njinjo asked.

"Yes, she paid me a visit not long ago with my son," Pa Taboh said.

Pa Njinjo turned to Pa Jamai and winked.

"Children of today!" he exclaimed. "They are like dogs, they go to places where you'd least expect them."

He said times had changed, adding that in his time, his father had chosen his wife without his knowledge and he had accepted without asking a single question.

"I don't say this in order to deny your son my daughter's hand. I'm only making sure that I will not be asked some day to refund a bride price because my daughter does not like the man to whom she has been betrothed," Pa Njinjo said.

In reponse, Pa Taboh said they had come as messengers. They had come strong in their belief that all was fine between their son and Pa Njinjo's daughter. He added that Tewuh was a very serious young man with great ambitions, and that he had no doubt at all that Pa Njinjo would be happy having him as son-in-law. After having said that, he turned to his eldest son who had carried a 20-liter jug of palm-wine and a bag of dried mud-fish and asked him to present the gifts to Natasha's father. The young man stood up briskly, heaved the jug of wine and fish and placed them in front of Pa Njinjo. Silence fell in the room again.

Pa Njinjo looked at the gifts, pulled his dark beard and looked at Pa Jamai.

"I can't touch these things without asking my wife to say something," Pa Njinjo said.

Having said that, he stepped out of the room and walked quickly to the room where the women were busy cooking food. He soon returned holding his wife by the hand.

"Mah Titi, these people here present have come to take your daughter Natasha away," Pa Njinjo said.

"Why? What have I done to them?" Mah Titi asked.

"They say their son is hungry and needs someone to cook his food for him," her husband said.

"Hmmmm!" she groaned.

"What do you have to tell them?" her husband asked again, looking into his wife's snake-like eyes.

"What do the men say? Whatever the men say would be acceptable to me," she said.

"That's good talk. You may return to the kitchen," he said.

As soon as she had turned her back Pa Njinjo stood up and made a short speech. He said he was in favor of the union between his daughter Natasha and Tewuh. He further said that the only concern he had was the ongoing hostilities between their two villages, adding that he fervently hoped that the marriage would bring an end to the ill-will that had marred relations between the hitherto sister villages.

"Before the rednecks came here, the people of Lohbeuhjia and those of Lohmeukoh lived together as brethren but the day the long noses set foot here, our troubles began," he said.

"You're quite right. The red feet came here and set brother against brother," Pa Taboh said.

Pa Jamai looked at both speakers and nodded his head in approbation.

"What we've done here today, will cement our brotherhood once again. We can't be so foolish as to let foreigners divide us," he said.

"Times are changing, and our children are leading the way toward reconciliation," Pa Taboh said.

"Our brothers have spoken well," said Pa Jamai.

He then proceeded to pour the palm-wine into the cup of Pa Njinjo. When it was full, he turned round and poured it into his own cup and then into everyone's cups. Given that Natasha was away, her youngest sister was called into the room and asked to pour palm-wine into the cup of Pa Taboh as a token of acceptance on behalf of her older sister. Everyone received a kola nut to chew with the wine. Pa Njinjo drank from his cup and gave it Pa Taboh who drank from it and gave it back to him. He took a second sip and called the mothers of Tewuh and Natasha from the kitchen. They came and drank from his cup and returned to cook.

When the cooking was over, the women brought food and served the men. They were all starving because the deliberations had lasted a long time. It was a sumptuous meal. The women ate their share in the kitchen. As soon as they had finished eating, Pa Njinjo brought beer, whisky and majunga to entertain his visitors who left at dusk all tipsy. It was a contented group of people that left Lohbeujia for Lohmeukoh that evening.

Natasha and Tewuh were elated when news about the success of the negotiations reached them at school. They were so excited that they went and drank too much beer at the campus tavern nicknamed 'Library'. Natasha was dead drunk when Tewuh opened her door and laid her on her bed. He locked the door and left to his own room.

They planned their marriage to coincide with their graduation from E.A.S. Natasha was already wearing Tewuh's diamond engagement ring. As soon as Tewuh returned home brandishing what he called his 'passport to the ivory tower of academia', his uncle asked him to invite his most reliable friends to accompany them to the home of Natasha. On the next mbingo[191] Tewuh and his parents left for Lohbeuhjia accompanied by a retinue of thirty-five men and women all in their early twenties to 'buy' Tewuh's wife. They hired two 14-seater buses for the trip. Tewuh's uncle had bought two huge rams and five head-cow[192] from the Mambim market.He had also bought ten jugs of palm-wine, five calabashes of raffia-wine, eight ten-liters of nkang[193] and three bottles of kwacha.[194] His mother assisted by her three daughters had prepared ten food-flasks of corn-fufu and njama-njama soup. Her two elder sisters had cooked bahcheukeuh and kwa-coco.Her younger brother brought five-liters of majunga.

It was a big crowd that entered the compound of Pa Njinjo on that day. In preparation for the occasion, he had asked Natasha and her younger sisters to sweep and clean the compound thoroughly. He had bought five crates of 33 Export, seven crates of Mutzik and two crates of Beaufort beer. He did not forget to buy

Becks beer, a brand reserved for political big shots and the wealthy. Natasha was the first of his daughters to get married. Her achievement called for a sumptuous feast. Natasha's mother was beaming with joy. At long last her younger daughters could now go out and hunt for their own partners, something they were forbidden to do until their oldest sister had found a husband.

When the visitors had assembled in the parlor of Pa Njinjo, he stood up, clapped his hands twice in reverence to the ancestors and welcomed his guests.

"My brothers and sisters, welcome! It is with a heart full of joy that I welcome you all to this compound again."

"*Ngeeeh! Ngeeeh keleeeh!*" the visitors responded.

"I hope that the sun that is shining in my heart is shining in yours too," he continued.

"*Habeeh! Habeeh!*" the visitors chorused.

"Today the gods of Ngoketu have decided to unite my family and yours."

"Wuuuuleeh! Wuuuuleeh! Wuuuuleeh!" they screamed.

"What the gods have put together, let no man or woman try to put asunder," he added.

"Wuulu Fongbobi! Wuulu Fongbombu!" the people concurred in unison.

"May the gods of Lohbeuhjia and those of Lohmeukoh cement the union between our children," he said and sat down.

"*Ndonyi! Ndonyi! Ndonyi!*" the crowd sang.

Thunderous applause greeted his speech, followed by a speech made by Tewuh's uncle.

"My dear brothers and sisters, needless to say that a good speech is sweeter than fresh palm-wine. I thank my brother for the wonderful speech he has made."

"Yeeleee! Yeeleee!" the people shouted.

"Poom! Poom!" sounded the gun of Pa Njinjo. He had fired two shots into the air to celebrate the marriage of his first daughter.

"A good wind blew us to this great compound. Yes, we knocked the good foot on our way to this home. And we give thanks to the gods of Ngoketu," he said.

"Noh sheung! Noh sheung!" the crowed went again.

"We're hungry and you gave us food," he said.

"Heung! Heung!" the hosts shouted.

"We're thirty and you quenched our thirst," he added.

"Uluuh! Uluuh! Uluuh!" the crowd screamed.

"We needed fertile land on which to plant our seeds and you gave us land."

"*Heeee! Heeee! Heee!*" people laughed, amused by the sexual innuendo in the statement.

"I add my mouth to that of my late brother, Kunta, to thank you all for your unbeatable generosity," he said, sitting down.

It was then time to negotiate the bride price. Tewuh and Natasha who had been kept away in an inner room were bought out to meet their prospective in-laws. After shaking hands and kissing the feet of all the visitors, they were asked to stand shoulder-to-shoulder in the middle of the room facing the door. They were both wearing the same type of outfit made out of elephant grass. They tied the peace plant on their left wrists. People were talking excitedly in hushed tones.

When calm returned, Pa Njinjo nodded to Pa Jamai who stood up, took three strides toward the couple and placed himself right in front of them. Raising his stentorian voice, he sang:

Ooh! Ooh! Ooh! Ooh!
Beunyi bah-lo! Ooh! Ooh!
Beechi vabong ndeuneuchi! Ooh! Ooh!
Beechi bong ndeubeuh tuh! Ooh! Ooh!
Ahoo! Hoo! Ahoo! Hoo!
Puum! Paam! Puum! Paam!
Ndoh Nyi! Ndoh Nyi!
Puum! Paam! Puum! Paam!

It was a song of propitiation to the gods of fertility. He was asking them to fertilize Natasha and Tewuh and bless them with as many children as possible. He was cursing the evil spirits who often fried the stomach of women thereby sowing seeds of discord in matrimonial homes. For who would keep a woman who does not bear children? He then handed the couple to Pa Njinjo's paternal aunt who led them back to the inner room where they were to remain until the negotiations were concluded.

Pa Njinjo asked the family of Tewuh to follow him to an adjacent room, reminding them that in their village people negotiating bride price don't have to sit in the same room. Natasha's relatives remained in the parlor. When Pa Njinjo was certain that his visitors were ready to receive the messenger, he sent his youngest brother with five hundred broom sticks to give Pa Taboh.These sticks represented the amount of money he wanted as dowry for his daughter. Each stick stood for 1 000 CFA francs. Pa

Taboh took the bundle, subtracted three hundred sticks and gave two hundred to the messenger to take to Pa Njinjo. He received the bundle, added two hundred sticks to it and gave it to the messenger to take to Pa Taboh. He received the bundle, subtracted one hundred sticks and sent back the bundle to Pa Njinjo. He received the bundle, added fifty sticks and sent it back to Pa Taboh, admonishing the messenger to not return. That was how the sum of three hundred and fifty thousand CFA francs was agreed upon as the price bride for Natasha.

Pa Njinjo invited his guests back into the parlor. Tewuh and Natasha also came out. As soon as they appeared, he gave his daughter a knotted rope and asked her to wear it on Tewuh's neck. She did. Pa Taboh then asked Tewuh's mother to offer the ndikong[195] cloth to Natasha's mother. She conformed. Next, Pa Njinjo asked his daughter to pour palm-wine into his ndeubeuh. She obeyed. He then asked her to place it on the lips of Tewuh to drink. She did as instructed. After Tewuh had drunk he was asked to place the cup on Natasha's lips to drink. As soon as she had drunk from the cup, the crowd went wild with jubilation. That was the sign of the consummation of marriage.

It was an elated crowd that left Lohbeuhjia that night for Lohmeukoh. Tewuh thanked everyone for a task well accomplished when they arrived at the Ntehnkah taxi rank. That night he slept soundly. He was a happy man. E.A.S had given him two trophies, namely a teaching qualification and a wife. Natasha had advised him against organizing a glamorous wedding party. Her reasoning was that they would need the money to get started in life. She told her husband that the kind of extravagant marriages for which bush-fallers[196] were notorious were wasteful. She said she had learned from friends living overseas that very often those kinds of marriages ended on the rocks on account of financial dire straits caused by credit card debts incurred for the purpose of ostentatious weddings at home.

Two days following the customary marriage, their families accompanied them to the Municipal office where Mayor Tabali pronounced them husband and wife and issued them a marriage certificate. A modest party with friends and family members followed at the Plaisir Bar.

9

They had no difficulty finding jobs. Tewuh who had gone to *Ecole Anormale Supérieure* on a private sponsorship from Saint Cassava High School went back to teach there. His wife had to be posted to a government high school because she was sponsored by the State. The only problem they encountered was having Natasha posted to a school in the Ndobo Area School District where her husband worked. Tewuh thought it would be wise to act sooner rather than later. They decided to make a trip to Edouany to chase her file. Not that they were doing anything out of the ordinary. In that country everyone chased files. If you wanted to be absorbed into the public service, you had to chase your file. If you had worked for two years without pay and wanted your salary to be paid, you chased your file. If you wanted the government to pay the arrears for those years you worked without pay you chased your file. If you went on retirement and had not received your pension for five years (which was often the case), you had to go to Edouany and chase your file. It was a nation of chasers. Whether you were chasing files, women or shadows, you were still a chaser.

They arrived in the city at 6:00pm having traveled for eight hours on a bus that stopped in very town and city to pick up passengers going to different destinations. They slept with a friend and left the following morning for the Ministry of the Public Service. As soon as they stepped out of the taxi their eyes fell on Paul Ndenge, a classmate of theirs at E.A.S.

"Bo! Massa, so na how?"[197]Ndenge said, giving Tewuh five.

"Bro, no be na we dis? Wata go lef stone,"[198] Tewuh said.

"Ah Natasha! How no moumie?"[199] Ndenge said, throwing his hands open for an embrace.

Natasha responded with a cold handshake.

"Massa, what brings you to Yaoundé?"Tewuh asked

"Chasing files, massa. Do you know that since we graduated six months ago everyone is still waiting for postings?" Ndenge said.

"Are you serious?" Tewuh asked, very surprised.

"Yes, what do I gain from telling a lie?" Ndenge said.

"Have you been posted? "Ndenge asked.

"My case is different," Tewuh said.

"Massa, I forgot that you're the son of a big shot," Ndenge said.

"Please, please. Who dash dog coat?[200] I am the son of poor farmers," Tewuh said.

"So what you do mean when you say your case is different?" Ndenge asked.

"I was on private sponsorship at E.A.S. So I have gone back to my job," Tewuh explained.

"So you're on study leave at E.A.S? Na youa own fain-oh?"[201] Ndenge said, looking at Tewuh with eyes full of envy.

"I arrived from Nkongsamba yesterday where I have been doing mbambe wok[202] and was shocked when the receptionist told me that the minister is still looking into the files of people who graduated from E.A.S. twelve months ago," Ndenge said.

"You must be joking!" Tewuh said clapping his hands.

"So, how do they expect people to survive?" Natasha asked.

"You think they really care about your survival?" Ndenge asked.

"What's the fate of recent graduates?" Tewuh asked.

"Your guess is as good as mine. They'll have to wait until their turn comes," Ndenge said.

He recounted how the Ministry of the Public Service had been converted into a rachet, explaining that some E.A.S. graduates who had been privately sponsored had worked their way onto government payroll by giving bribes. Others had refused to take up their duties in remote parts of the country. They had simply stayed in the city and continued to earn their salaries for no work done. He said he knew of E.A.S graduates who were earning salaries from the government while teaching in private schools.

"Bro, dis kontri na wa-oh!"[203] Tewuh said, yawning.

"It's a shame, my friend. How can people govern their own country as if they're strangers helping themselves to manna from heaven?" Ndenge asked.

"It's unbelievable! It's feels like we're living in a nation taken hostage," Natasha said.

"Massa, it was nice talking to you guys. I must be going," Ndenge said.

"Thanks man, we're going into the building to see what they have in store for us," Tewuh said.

"Good luck with the wahala[204]," Ndenge said.

"Bye Ndenge," Natasha said.

"Bye now," he said.

Tewuh and Natasha walked into the Ministry and heard four female Anglophones talking in angry tones in front of a receptionist. They did not recognize any of them but approached them because they were speaking English. Tewuh greeted them and asked them if they were there for posting. One of the women, looking as if had been crying, said she was posted two and half years ago. When Tewuh asked why she was in Yaoundé, she said she was chasing her integration file. She explained that she had not received a dime from the government since she took up a teaching position in Belabo.

"How do you survive without a salary?" Tewuh asked.

"God alone knows, my brother," the woman said morosely.

"So what prevents them from paying your salary?" Natasha asked.

"I wish I knew, my sister," she said.

"Are you here for the same matter," asked the second woman who was pregnant.

"We've not even been posted yet," Natasha said.

"What difference does it make? Posted or not, you still go on an empty stomach," the third woman said, wiping sweat from her wrinkled face.

"If you are here for posting, there is the door to knock on," the lady said, pointing at the door painted gray.

"Thank you so much, and good luck!" Natasha said.

As Tewuh and Natasha walked through a hall he recalled what had happened to him there the first time he was in that building. Memories of the scuffle he had with Francophone aggressors flooded his mind. Cold sweat ran down his spine and he remained quiet for some time. His wife asked him if he was fine and he said he was okay. They knocked on the door and a male voice answered from within.

"*Entrez s'il vous plaît!*"

They had taken an elementary French course at E.A.S. and understood that the man was asking them to come in. They gently pushed open the door, went in and said 'good morning' to a tall fair-complexioned man dressed in a three-piece charcoal gray suit sitting behind a mahogany table full of files.

"*Veuillez vous asseoir,*" he said, which could be translated as "Please have a seat".

The word "*asseoir*" sounded familiar. They sat down on chairs facing the man. A name plate on the table read: "Johnson

Epie, Secrétaire d'état, which could be translated as "Johnson Epie, Secretary of State.

"*Comment puis-je vous aider?*"[205] the man said.

"Sir, we are Anglophones. We can't speak French. Could you maybe speak to us in English?" Tewuh said.

"*Madame et Monsieur, je ne comprends pas votre patois-là hein! Si vous ne parlez pas français, je n'y peux rien*[206]," Johnson Epie said.

"But sir, aren't you Anglophone by any chance? When I read Epie on your name plate, I thought I'd met a brother from the South-West Province," Tewuh said.

The man lost his temper and spoke at the top of his voice.

"*Monsieur, si vous êtes venu ici chercher des ennuis je vous mettrai dehors tout de suite!*"

As soon as he had said this, he went back to his files. A little while later his phone rang. He picked it up and started to speak in Bakossi.When the conversation ended he put down his phone and stared into the eyes of his visitors as if he was trying to read something on their faces. Suddenly he said:

"Look, I'm going to do something I normally don't do. I'll speak to you in English but don't go out there and start to announce to everyone that Epie is an Anglophone. They know me here as a Francophone," he said, blinking like a thief caught in the act.

"We'll keep our mouths sealed, sir," Tewuh said, thanking him.

"How may I help you?"

"My wife here present, graduated from E.A.S. four months ago and hasn't been posted yet," Tewuh said.

"Ha! Ha! Ha!" Epie burst into laughter.

"It's not a joke, sir," Tewuh said, not knowing why the man was laughing.

"I'm not laughing because it's funny. Things don't work here the way you imagine,"Epie said.

He went into a lengthy explanation of how files do not move by themselves. He said someone had to push them. When Tewuh said he did not know the way things worked there he laughed again uproariously.

"There's another problem, sir," Tewuh said.

"What's the problem?" Epie asked.

"I work in Ndobo in the North-West Province and would like to have my wife posted to a school near me," Tewuh said.

"That requires two people to push her file," Epie said.

"So are you going to help us?" Tewuh asked.

"If you speak well," Epie said.

"What does that mean?" Tewuh asked.

"People who push files, normally get their palms greased. Aren't you Cameroonian?" he asked.

"Of course, I am, sir," Tewuh said, trying hard to conceal his anger.

"You don't act like one," Epie said.

"I don't mean to offend you, sir, but you speak in proverbs. Could you be explicit?" Tewuh asked.

Without looking at his visitors, Epie said it would cost them the sum of two hundred and fifty thousand CFA francs to have Natasha posted immediately. To ensure that she is posted to the Ndobo Area School District, it would cost an additional one hundred and fifty thousand CFA francs.

"Thank you, Mr Epie. I know what you're driving at. You want a bribe! That's what Cameroonians are good at, bribery and corruption! I'll make sure this message goes beyond this office," Tewuh said, slamming the door behind him. Natasha was after him telling him to calm down.

Tewuh was very upset. He had been living with the illusion that the people fuelling the corruption machine in the country were Francophones. Little did he know that his Anglophone brothers and sisters were equally corrupt. Worse still, they're suffering from an identity crisis. Here was a Bakossi man passing for a Francophone.

"It that what it takes to be Ongolan, honey?" he asked his wife.

"I don't know, dear," Natasha said, not wanting to make things worse.

Tewuh continued to talk to himself. I will never wear a mask. Never! Never deny myself! Never sell my heritage for pieces of copper. Never! If Ongola did not want him because he was Anglophone, he was going to leave. He would go away to other climes and live by other chimes. He was tired of being treated like an underdog. He was fed up with being called a second-class citizen in his own country.

Natasha was equally cross with Epie but did not approve of what she saw as an overreaction on the part of her husband.

"Honey, maybe we should have negotiated. He might have settled for a smaller amount," she said.

"Honey, that's not the point. If you start giving bribes in this country, there'll be no end to it," he said.

"Take it easy. God is in control," she said.

"God is on vacation is this blighted nation!" he said.

"Calm down, darling. Let's keep God out of this business. Where are we going?" she asked.

"To Bamenda," Tewuh said.

They arrived in Bamenda at 10:30pm and boarded a clando taxi to Ndobo. While they were in bed, Natasha told her husband that she would like to go to the village and talk to her father about the problem they were facing regarding her posting. She said her father had a few business partners there who may be able to help. Tewuh said it was fine with him as long as it did not require them to give bribes.

When day broke, Natasha left for Lohbeuhjia while her husband was still asleep. She arrived at home when her father and mother were eating breakfast. The inquiring looks they had on their faces made her feel that they did not expect her.

"Is there trouble in your husband's house?" her father asked.

"No, why?" she asked.

"What brings our baby here so early in the morning?" her mother asked.

"So you thought I'd gone for good? Once a baby always a baby," she said, grinning.

"We are glad to see you. You look pregnant," her father said.

"How did you know, dad?" she asked, surprised at her father's perspicacity.

"Thank God! God has blessed the union!" he said, hugging his daughter.

"Praise to the Almighty! Soon I'll be a grandmother! He's an awesome God. May He continue to bless you with more children," her mother prayed rubbing her stomach with both her hands.

"So what brings you? I'm leaving to Ndumbu for business," her father said.

"Dad, I have something to discuss with you," she said.

"What's the matter, dear?" he asked.

Natasha told him that they had been having a difficult time in Yaoundé trying to get her posting. She said she would love to work in Ndobo near her husband but so far things had proven to be impossible. She recounted their encounter with the Secretary of

State for the Public Service and told her father that the meeting had ended unsuccessfully because he had asked for a bribe.

Pa Njinjo assured her daughter that he would do everything possible to make sure things turned out the way she wanted. He said, his friend, Polycarp Mjindum, a member of parliament for the Chop Pipo Dem Moni (CPDM) party was a very influential man and would help if he asked him for help.

"Honorable Mjindum is a very reliable person. I will be in touch with him when I return from Ndumbu. If he needs papers from you I'll let you know. Don't worry my daughter," he said, patting her on the back.

The MP he was taking about was a semi-illiterate who had served a prison term at the Kondengui Maximum Security prison for alleged involvement in massive misappropriation of funds at CENADI in Yaoundé. After his release from jail he had worked his way back into the same job and eventually into the National Assembly through electoral fraud masterminded by the party in power. He was one of those handclapping MP's who knew nothing about the spirit and letter of the law. Like many of his peers, he slept throughout parliamentary sessions and earned a fabulous salary at the end of the month.

Tewuh returned from school and found his wife vomiting. Scared, he rushed her to the Obing-Obing Hospital for a medical check-up. After examining her thoroughly the doctor on duty told Tewuh that his wife was in good health and attributed her throwing up to the journey she had made on a bumpy road that day.

They had been waiting for three months when one day they heard Natasha's name read on Radio-One-Battery during the Luncheon Date Program. She had been posted to the Government Bilingual High School in Ndobo and was being asked to report for duty without further delay. They were very happy and prayed her salary would go through and follow soon.

Natasha began to teach that same week. Her colleagues were very friendly. The principal Dr Ndutuh did everything he could to make her baptism of fire as hitch-free as possible. The students were well behaved and called her "auntie" even though they were not biologically related to her. As her pregnancy grew bigger she started to notice certain changes in her body and appetite. She frequently had swollen legs and had the urge to spit constantly. She carried an empty bottle into which she spat. She also took to eating white clay. At times, she would feel as if two little kids were running around playing soccer in her stomach.

Tewuh's mother took proper care of her, educating her on the importance of child care, especially breast-feeding. At times Natasha's abdominal pains hurt so much that she would lie down on the bare floor weeping. Her mother-in-law would come and sit beside her consoling her and telling her it would soon be over. One night as they were about to go to bed, Natasha's pains became unbearable. She felt like going to the toilet but each time she went, nothing came out. The noise in her stomach was like the sound of a blacksmith's bellow blowing fire. Tewuh got up from his chair and went to call his mother. They rushed Natasha to the local maternity. Two hours later she gave birth to twins girls.

That momentous event was going to change the lives of both parents dramatically. In their culture twins were considered extraordinary children endowed with supernatural powers. For that reason, they were treated with particular care. They were given special names as soon as they were born. The first was called Bitie and the second Bunkwe.Their babysitters were named Leghu and Mbiayuh. According to the mores of the land, Tewuh and Natasha were also given special names. Tewuh added the title Chui to his names and Natasha added Tohnjeuh to hers.

Soon after Natasha's return home with her babies, a fence made up of wet sticks and palm fronds was constructed around the house where the children and parents were to going to live. The purpose of the fence was to keep away visitors. The parents were subjected to certain restrictions. For example, they were prohibited from drinking *egusi* soup. They could not visit a compound where someone had died and had recently been buried. They could not touch a corpse. Each time they went out to visit friends or family members they were obligated to hold the 'peace plant' in their hands. They were not allowed to wash, shave or comb their hair until the children were a year old.

Tewuh and his wife found those restrictions very daunting, especially given that they were teachers. Consequently, they decided to go to the Fon's palace and plead their case. The Fon listened to them patiently until they had finished saying what they had to say. Then he asked them one question.

"Have you ever seen a river flowing up a mountain?"

"No, Mbeh," Chui Tewuh answered.

"Why then do you want to change our customs? These traditions were handed to us by our forebears. We've got to keep them," the Fon said, staring at them.

"Mbeh, the problem is that we're teachers. How do we stand in front of children with unkempt hair and peace plants in our hands?" Tewuh asked.

"There's nothing wrong with that! Everyone has a culture. You don't have to change your culture because of students; they too have native traditions," the Fon said, adjusting the shia boloh[207] on his oblong head.

"We hear you, Mbeh," Tewuh said.

"Go well, my children. And don't forget that any member of your family who has had sex shouldn't see or touch your children for three days," the Fon advised.

Chui Tewuh and his wife were very disappointed with the outcome of their visit to the palace. They realized that they could not change tradition. Natasha suggested that they should take up the issue with their respective principals. Chui Tewuh's boss was a kind man and gave him permission to comply with tradition. He said he would let the students know that he was going through a rite of passage. His students loved him and did not care. Many of them were sons and daughters of the soil and were familiar with the custom.

Conversely, Tohnjeuh Natasha had difficulty convincing her French-born principal to allow her come to class with disheveled hair and a plant in her hand. He argued that it was against the principles of public instruction to use the classroom as a forum for showcasing indigenous cultures and beliefs. After a lengthy argument he decided to place her on a three-month maternity leave, pointing out that she must come to class after that period or look for a substitute teacher and pay out of her pocket. She talked the issue over with her husband and they agreed to hire a substitute teacher at the end of her leave.

That decision and the extra demands of childcare created dents in their shoe-string budgets. To alleviate the financial burden, Chui Tewuh decided to take up a part-time job with a local opposition weekly newspaper, *Drum.* He wrote a Monday column titled 'Voice of the Voiceless' in which he x-rayed the shortcomings of the party in power. In one of his scathing articles titled 'Manufacturing the Illusion of Freedom', he lashed out at the ineptitude of President Paul Sit-Tight calling him a lame duck who kept his country in perpetual bondage by playing politics of the ostrich. He questioned the rationale behind keeping Ongola in economic bondage through adherence to the Franc Zone, arguing that the devaluation of the CFA franc was having devastating economic consequences on the lives of the citizenry. He ended the article by describing the Head of State as a minion whose only achievement since his accession to power more than twenty years ago was to line his pockets and buy real estate in France and Baden-Baden.

The write-up brought Chui Tewuh into a head-on collision with the nation's belligerent regime. As soon as the newspaper hit the newsstands he was kidnapped by State security agents, who took him to an unknown destination. He was physically assaulted and tortured. Within a few hours, news of his kidnapping was the talk of the town. His friends had called Radio Tisong to report his kidnapping which was immediately broadcast. Embarrassed by the news, State security agents released Chui Tewuh. No explanation was provided as to why he was kidnapped or who the brain was behind the kidnapping.

From that day he knew that he was a wanted man in the land of his birth. His twins were then one year old and his wife was pregnant with their third child. They had to perform the traditional rites for the release of the twins from the fence. Assisted by his mother, uncle, and parents-in-law, he organized the ceremony. He invited other twin parents in the village. His mother bought several bunches of plantains, tins of palm-oil, meat and smoked mud-fish. Pa Taboh bought many bags of table-salt. There was plenty of palm-wine and beer to drink.

As soon as the guests were seated on freshly made bamboo chairs inside the fenced house, Chui Tewuh and Tohnjeuh Natasha stood up, greeted everyone and thanked them for coming. They then started to share the plantains, salt, and palm-oil among the parents of older twins in the village. When they had finished their task, a pair of selected twin mothers stood up and sang a special song in honor of the young twins who were about to graduate from the fence:

> Wuli! Wuli! Wuli!
> Bitie! Bunkwe!
> Vasheubi noh beuloh!
> Weeyee! Weeyee! Weeyee!
> Teuki noh beukeuh!
> Weeyee! Weeyee! Weeyee!
> Beetieeh nduoh! Beetieeh nduoh!

Wuli! Wuli! Wuli!

The singing went on interminably while Chui Tewuh and Tohnjeuh Natasha had been made to sit on the stalk of a banana tree placed in the middle of the room. An elderly twin mother came forward holding a sharpened knife in her right hand and clean shaved them both. This brought the ceremony to an end. Three gunshots were fired by Tewuh's uncle and the fence was torn apart by a group of young men. Feasting started and ended at dusk.

That night Chui Tewuh's sleep was interrupted by a dream in which he was in communion with his deceased father. The phantom was saying to him: Flee! Flee! Flee, my son! He started to play the American green card lottery.

10

When news broke that Chui Tewuh and his wife Tohnjeuh Natasha had won the green card lottery, they became the hottest news items around town. Their names were on every lip in the village of Ndobo. Everyone wanted to know what they would be doing in the United States of America. Their relatives wanted to know where they would live and what they would eat in the white man's land. Others were interested in finding out whether their teenage children would be able to make friends with white kids. Some poor relatives came holding their caps and headscarves in their hands asking for their own share of the lottery money.

"Ma pikin, gibe ma own moni mek I tchop before die take me go,"[208] Tewuh's maternal aunt said, stretching her headscarf in front of her nephew.

"Auntie, dis green card lottery wey I chop'am so no be moni,"[209] Chui Tewuh explained.

"Ah ah! If lotta no be moni, na wheti no ma pikin? I beg gibe ma own mek I de go me nayo-nayo,"[210] the woman said.

"Auntie, *you be* ma mami. I no fit lie you, lottery na daso half book wey gomna for America gibe me mek I take'am enter for America,"[211] Chui Tewuh explained.

"Mof-me-de!" Wona tchotchoro dem wona sabe wayo pass mark![212] the seventy-two-year-old emaciated woman exclaimed in desperation.

"My son, will there be a furnished home waiting for you and your wife when you arrive in America?" Pa Taboh asked his nephew, a grin of contentment on his heart-shaped face.

"No uncle, we'll have to rent or buy our own house," Chui Tewuh said.

"Oh! Is that true?"

"Yes, uncle," Chui Tewuh assured his uncle.

"This story is bigger than my head. So what is this green card lottery?"

"Uncle, the green card is only a visa, an authorization that allows my wife, my children, and me to immigrate to the United States of America.

"Alright! I thought our suffering was now a thing of the past now that you've won the lottery," the sexagenarian said.

"No, uncle. Money may come but we'll have to work for it," Chui Tewuh explained.

"Is there a job waiting for you in the white man's country?" Chui Tewuh's mother asked.

"No, mama. We'll have to look for our own jobs," her son answered.

"This I don't understand. You have a good job here, why go to a strange land to look for work?" his mother asked.

"I hear that America is the land of dreams," Chui Tewuh explained.

"Land of dreams, my son? So when you sleep here you don't dream?" his mother asked, worried.

"Mama, what I mean is that in America, everyone can succeed. You don't need to speak French or give bribes to get a job," Chui Tewuh said, smiling contentedly.

"Mama, America is a land of opportunities. It is good for these children," Tohnjeuh Natasha cut in.

"Wheti wona go chop for dat farway kontri? Dem de cook fufu-corn wet njama-njama for deh?" [213] Tewuh's paternal grandmother asked.

"No grandma, fufu wet njama-njama no de for deh but we no go die hungry. Mukala dem no de sleep wet hungry. Chop de for deh. We hear say dem get hamburger wet hot-dog mberekete," [214]Chui Tewuh explained.

"Eeeh! Eeeh! Da pipo dem de chop dog!"[215] the ninety-one-year-old woman exclaimed, clapping her cupped hands thrice in disbelief.

Silence fell on the crowd that had assembled that evening to wish Chui Tewuh and his family farewell to the dream-land. Chui Tewuh's oldest uncle who had served in the colonial army in England advised him not to throw away the chance of a life time.

"Take a chance, my son. You may never have this opportunity again. Life belongs to those who venture. A sedentary snake never looks fresh," the elderly man said.

After having said this, he invited everyone to join him in pouring libation. Standing up bare body except for a sanja[216] tied around his tiny waist he uttered the following incantations:

Gods of mbolo, gods of messi, gods of mbongkoh
Goddesses of nguala, goddesses of meusoh,
Goddesses of Bekeu, and goddesses of Teuloh,

We place our son, daughter, and their children in your hands. Watch over them day and night. Protect them from strong heat, from biting cold, from thunder storms, and from hailstones. Be their eyes and ears everywhere they go in the land of the long noses. Help them to understand the language of birds spoken over there. Provide them with good food to eat. We don't want our children to eat dogs like the white man. Give them clean water to drink. For this we pray in the name of our ancestors who have gone before us to live forever. Yie Nyi.[217]

The next day Tewuh and Tohnjeuh Natasha boarded an opep[218] bound for Yaoundé. They had to attend an immigrant visa interview at the American embassy after going through a medical examination with Dr Ben Nnamu, the only Anglophone physician in the entire nation certified to perform these tests. The couple arrived in Yaoundé late in the evening and passed the night with a village friend who works there.

"Massa! God don really butter wona bread-oh!"[219] Londu said, slapping the palm of Chui Tewuh.

"Bo, no be na daso goodlok,"[220] Chui Tewuh said, smiling from ear to ear.

"So how's everyone doing back in the village?"

"Everyone is doing very well. I saw your folks before leaving. They said I should extend their greetings to you," Chui Tewuh said.

"Massa, my folks didn't even think of sending me some miondo[221] and fried groundnuts from the village? You know those things are scarce here," Londu said, laughing uproariously.

"Bo, it's our fault. We informed them about our trip late last night. It was too late for them to prepare something for you. We apologize," Chui Tewuh said.

"No problem, my friend. I know how excited you both are to go to America. At moments like these, one may even forget his wife," Londu said, laughing loudly.

"I hear you, my friend. Take this, it is our gift to you", Chui Tewuh said, giving his friend a bundle of bunga.

"Thank you, thank you, eeh! My number six[222] told me that you had something sweet from the village for me."

"We thank God," Tohnjeuh Natasha said.

"So tomorrow you will go to Dr Nnamu's laboratories for the medical examination and then head for the American embassy, right?" Londu asked.

"Yes, that's what we'll do tomorrow," Chui Tewuh said, wishing his friend good night.

The next morning the couple took a taxi to Dr Nnamu's laboratories located at Nkolbison. They did not eat breakfast as stated in the documents they had received from America. After paying their medical consultation fees of 65, 000 CFA francs each at the cash registry, they were asked to go in and meet the specialist.

"I will examine your wife first, you can wait outside," Dr Nnamu said to Chui Tewuh.

"Breath in, breath out," the physician said, running his stethoscope over the woman's chest and back.

"Have you ever had a miscarriage?"

"No, doctor."

"Have you ever contracted a sexually transmitted disease?"

"No, doctor."

"Promiscuity is an evil."

"Yes, doctor."

"Have you ever aborted a pregnancy?"

"No, doctor."

"Life is precious."

"Yes, doctor."

"I'm done, you can get dressed. You'll be given your results in a half hour. Ask your husband to come in," he said to Tohnjeuh Natasha.

"Thank you, doctor."

"You may hang your clothes over there, sir," the doctor said pointing to a hanger.

"Thank you, doctor."

"Have you ever smoked?" Dr Nnamu asked, looking at Chui Tewuh's blackened lips.

"Yes, doctor", he said, biting his lower lips.

"How long?"

"Five years, doctor."

"Do you smoke now?"

"No, doctor."

"Good! Do you drink alcohol?"

"Yes, doctor."

"What do you drink?"

"Jobajo."

"How much?"

"Ten or twelve bottles a day."

"*Wew!* Alcohol kills."

"Yes, doctor."

"Have you ever had a sexually transmitted disease?"

"Yes, doctor."

"What was it you had?"

"Gonorrhea, doctor."

"Was it successfully treated?"

"Yes, doctor."

"Is there anything else you would like me to know about your health?"

"No, doctor."

"I'm done, you may get dressed. Your results will be ready in a half hour."

"Thank you, doctor."

Chui Tewuh was shivering as he came out of the doctor's consultation room. The 28-year-old man was so scared he looked forty. It was clear that he was unsure of the outcome of the medical examination. After thirty minutes, a short sturdy woman wearing abundant lipstick came out of the room adjacent to the doctor's.

"Mr. Chui Tewuh!" she called.

"Present, madam", he answered like a school child.

"Here are your results, sir. Take them to the American embassy. Do not tamper with the seal on the envelope."

"Thank you, madam," Chui Tewuh said, holding his envelope tight in his quivering hands.

"Mrs. Tohnjeuh Natasha!" The woman called.

"I'm here, madam."

"Here are your results, ma'am. Take them to the American embassy. Do not mess with the seal on the envelope."

"Thank you, madam," Tohnjeuh Natasha said, following her husband out of the building.

"What do you think of the examination?" she asked, throwing her lanky hands round his long neck.

"My dear, I don't know. Let's just take the results to the embassy and hear what they'll say," Chui Tewuh said with a look of apprehension on his heart-shaped face.

"May I see your identity papers please," a security guard asked them as they approached the door leading to the office of the consular officer.

"Here, sir," Chui Tewuh said, producing his national identity card and his wife's.

"Stand in this line. You'll be called in when it's your turn," the guard said.

Chui Tewuh kept stamping his swollen feet on the ground out of impatience. They had been waiting for four hours.

"Which kind barlok be dis-eh!"[223] He said to his wife.

"I sabi sei na wheti?"[224] his wife said.

After standing in the sun for five hours Chui Tewuh and Tohnjeuh Natasha were told by the security guard to go in.

"Are you Chui Tewuh?" the consular officer asked.

"Yes, sir," Chui Tewuh answered, trying to control himself.

"And this is your wife, Tohnjeuh Natasha. Is that correct?"

"That's correct, sir," Chui Tewuh replied.

"May I see your medical papers, please?"

"Here, sir," Chui Tewuh said, giving the consular officer the two sealed envelopes.

"Please, sit down," he said, opening the envelopes one after the other.

Chui Tewuh took a quick look at the huge poster behind the iroko table behind which the white man was sitting. It was the portrait of the Statue of Liberty on which were inscribed the words 'Land of the free' and 'Home of the brave'. These words whetted Chui Tewuh's appetite to taste of the good life in America.

"Hummm…," the officer said, his eyes riveted on Tohnjeuh Natasha's medical results.

"Is there a problem, sir?" Chui Tewuh asked quaking like a cocoyam leaf in a whirlwind.

"There's a huge problem," the officer said, taping his pen on the table.

"What's the problem, sir?" Chui Tewuh asked, breathlessly.

"Your wife has contracted a disease," the white man said.

"What kind of disease do I have, sir?" Tohnjeuh Natasha asked, closing her eyes despondently.

"The medical results show that you have a disease called Africanosomiasis," the officer said, poring over her papers.

"Oh, oh! Papa God, where are you? Come to my rescue! What have I done wrong to you!" the woman sobbed.

"Gentleman, I'm afraid your wife will not accompany you to the United States at present," the officer said.

Chui Tewuh fell from the chair on which he was sitting, crying as if he'd lost both his parents. His wife fell on him and they both threw themselves on the white man's feet asking to be pitied.

"Lady and gentleman, you don't have to do this. I'm not denying your wife the right to immigrate to America. As soon as she is cured of her disease she will be able to follow you to the US," the officer said to Chui Tewuh.

"How long will that take, sir?" We have three children! Help us, sir!" Chui Tewuh begged in tears.

"I don't know how long it will take to cure this disease, and there's nothing I can do at this point to help her. Mr. Chui Tewuh here's your immigrant visa to America. Your wife will be given hers whenever she's cured," he said, asking them to leave.

The six-hour return trip to Ndobo was mournful. Chui Tewuh did not utter a word to his wife until they arrived at their home.

"Tomorrow we are going to see Dr Wanki," he said to his wife.

"Why?" his wife asked.

"To find out what caused this illness and what can be done to cure it as quickly as possible," he said looking at his wife helplessly.

"Alright," Tohnjeuh Natasha replied dejectedly.

The following day they were the first in front of Dr Wanki's consultation room. After waiting for two hours, a svelt nurse came out holding a register in her left hand.

"Tohnjeuh Natasha here?" she said at the top of her shrill voice.

"Yes, madam," Tohnjeuh Natasha replied.

"Come in, please."

"My husband is here. May he come along?"

"No problem at all."

The couple went in and sat on cane-chairs in front of the Doctor.

"What can I do for you, lady and gentleman?"

"Doctor, we have a serious problem," Chui Tewuh said.

"What is it?" The choppy doctor asked wiping sweat from a forehead that looked like that of a ram.

We've just returned from Yaoundé where we were invited to attend an immigrant visa interview at the American embassy," Chui Tewuh said.

"Did you get the visa?"

"Yes, doctor. I got the visa...euh," Chui Tewuh said.

"Congratulations!" Dr Wanki cut in.

"Doctor, my wife did not get hers."

"Why not?"

"The consular officer said she had contracted a disease."

"What type of disease has she contracted?"

"Africanosomiasis," Chui Tewuh said.

"Goodness gracious! That's a dangerous one," Dr Wanki said.

"That's why we're here, doctor. We want to find out what causes this disease and how soon it can be cured."

"Africanosomiasis is contracted by eating white clay, especially by pregnant women. Patients react to treatment differently. In some cases it may take two years," the doctor explained.

"God Almighty! What have I done wrong? I'll kill myself! There's no use living," Tohnjeuh Natasha said, dancing up and down the doctor's room like someone suffering from diarrhea.

"Calm down! Calm down! You can't kill yourself because of a visa to America," Dr Wanki said to Tohnjeuh Natasha.

"Do you remember ever eating white clay?' he asked.

"Yes. When I was pregnant with my third child I ate a lot of that stuff. It was caused by the pregnancy. I couldn't stop eating it," Tohnjeuh Natasha said.

"Here is a prescription for your wife, sir," the doctor said, giving Chui Tewuh a sheet of white paper on which he had written the names of several drugs to be purchased.

Thank you very much, doctor," Chui Tewuh said, wiping his tears with a red handkerchief.

"As I said, this may take a very long time. Come see me after six months," Dr Wanki said.

"Goodbye doctor," Chui Tewuh said, holding his wife by the hand as they slowly walked out of the doctor's consultation room.

When Chui Tewuh got home he took out his immigrant visa and checked the expiration date.

"This visa will expire in six months," he said, looking into his wife's eyes.

"Is that correct?"

"Yes, look at it," he said, putting the visa into Tohnjeuh Natasha's hands.

"This is terrible!" she said, not knowing what else to say.

"My dear, I'm going to make a suggestion. I know you're sick but we can't afford to miss the chance of a lifetime. Let me go to America. You will follow me with our children once you're cured of this disease. I'll get a good job in America and send you money for your medications and food for the kids. We have a home, so you need not worry about rents," Chui Tewuh said, holding his head in his both hands.

"Alright, what can I say? If I can't go, at least you should go," Tohnjeuh Natasha said hopelessly.

A week later, Chui Tewuh packed his bags and boxes, wished his wife and children well and headed for the Douala International Airport. He had resigned from his job at Saint Cassava High School. At the airport the immigration police told him he couldn't go to America.

"Sir, your passport is invalid. You cannot go to the United States," the fat police constable said.

"Is my passport invalid?"

"Yes, sir. This passport is invalid," the officer insisted.

"I don't understand. I made this document only a month ago. If you want me to tchoko, just say so, chef[225]," Chui Tewuh said, taking out a five thousand CFA francs note and squeezing it into the palm of the police constable.

Without looking at it, he pushed it back into Chui Tewuh's palm.

"Mr. Chui Tewuh, the fiscal stamp in your passport has expired. If you want to go to America, give me two hundred thousand CFA francs," the constable said, frowning and gnashing his uneven teeth.

"Chef, I don't have two hundred thousand CFA francs," Chui Tewuh said, opening his wallet.

"Give me all the American dollars I see there. Je m'enfous!"[226] the constable said.

"No chef, I can't give you this money. I will need it on my arrival in America," Chui Tewuh said.

"Well, if I don't get all that money, you are not going to America. The ball is in your court. Tu paies, I lef you go. Tu ne paies pas, you lef for ya!"[227] the policeman said refusing to stamp Chui Tewuh's passport.

Sensing that talk wouldn't help, Chui Tewuh reluctantly pulled out the ten twenty-dollar bills he had in his wallet and handed them over to the constable.

"You may go, sir," he said putting the money in the chest pocket of his uniform.

Chui Tewuh grabbed his two boxes and handbag, left the police check-point, and headed for the Swiss Air waiting-room. After two hours, check-in started. Chui Tewuh presented his passport and visa and was about to board the aircraft when an airlines official ran after him.

"Sir, could you come back to the check-in room for a moment?"

"Me?"

"Yes, sir."

"What's the matter?" Chui Tewuh asked, trying to suppress his anger.

"It won't be long, sir," the officer said.

Frustrated, Chui Tewuh followed him.

"Could I take a look into your handbag?" the officer said when they got back to the check-in.

"No problem."

"What's this?" The white man said holding up the horn of a buffalo decorated with cowries and porcupine quills.

"Dis mukala dem di craze for dem head[228]. That's my ndong[229] sir," he said.

"What's inside?"

"Medication for stomach ache, sir."

"It looks like poison. It's so black."

"No, that's not poison sir," Chui Tewuh said, dipping his finger into the ndong and licking it.

"You may go but make sure you don't poison anyone in America," the officer said, giving the ndong back to Tewuh.

"Dis mukala dem na mbut,"[230] he said, putting his juju back into his handbag.

After being airborne for eighteen hours, Chui Tewuh arrived at the O'Hare International Airport in Chicago tired and hungry. The hustle and bustle of the city struck him dumb. Cars drove past at a maddening speed. People talked nonchalantly at the top of their voices.

"Luki, how do you guys manage to drive in a busy city like this?" He asked his friend who had come to pick him up.

"You get used to it with time. This is America, *Bro*. Welcome to the United States."

"Thank you my friend. I'm glad to be here," Chui Tewuh said, smiling broadly.

"Where are your kids and their mother?"

"Bro, na long long tory. I go tell you when we done reach ya long,"[231] Tewuh reverted to Pidgin English, a lingo he manipulated with ease.

When they got to his friend's flat he told him the story of his wife's illness.

"Massa, dem say ma woman get some sick wey dem de call'am Africanosomiasis,"[232] Chui Tewuh said.

"Is that why she couldn't come with you?"

"Yes," Chui Tewuh said, tears welling in his brown eyes.

"I'm sorry to hear that."

"Massa, na small ndole dis wey I bring'am mek you take ya smell for kontri,"[233] Chui Tewuh said giving his friend a bundle of green leaves from home.

"No! No! My man, I don't eat stuff like that anymore. It stinks. My wife will divorce me if she finds that stuff in this house," Luki said, putting the ndole away in his garage.

"Is your wife African?" Chui Tewuh asked.

"No, she's American," Luki said.

"I see. She doesn't eat African food?" Chui Tewuh asked.

"Bo, where do you find African food in America? In America, we eat American," Luki said, rubbing his close-cropped head.

"Where's your wife?"

"She's at work. In America everyone works. Two pay checks per family is way to go here," Luki said.

"Massa, no be yi better pass kontri?"[234] Chui Tewuh asked.

"Man, how can you compare apples and bananas? This is paradise!"

"No be na daso tory? How man fit take heaven begin measure'am wet hell."[235]

Their conversation was interrupted by the arrival of Megan, Luki's wife, who came in carrying boxes of spaghetti, pizza, and noodles.

"Welcome honey," Luki said, kissing his wife on her round lips.

"How was your day, honey?" she asked, throwing her delicate hands over her husband's raised shoulders.

"Good. Honey, meet our friend, Chui Tewuh from Africa," Luki said.

"Hello Mr. Chui Tewuh! Nice to meet you!" the tall lanky blonde, said without looking at her guest.

"Hello Mrs. Luki!" Chui Tewuh said.

"Call me Megan. I'm not Mrs. Luki," she said, blushing.

For two hours Luki prepared dinner while Megan relaxed on a couch reading a pornographic novel.

~ 112 ~

"Massa, na so wona own woman dem dei for hie?"[236]

"Wheti you mean, no?[237] Luki asked, resorting to Pidgin English in order to keep his wife out of the conversation.

"How titi go nang for chair na massa de cook dammer, no?"[238]

"Bo, you go for Rome, mek you do how wey pipo for Rome dem de do'am."[239]

"Massa, I ya you but I mimba say dis kain marred no go waka."[240]

"Wheda yi waka or yi no waka, palava dey? No be na daso marred for doki?"[241]

"Marred for doki na which one no, bo?"[242]

"Marred for doki na di one wey you take American nga put'am for youa long forseka sei yi go helep you mek you get youa green card quick-quick."[243]

"Oh! Ho! Dis palava don pass me!"[244] Tewuh shouted, laughing loudly.

"What does your friend find so funny, honey?" Megan asked.

"Don't mind him honey, he's been like this since childhood. Please come to the table, food is ready," Luki invited his friend and wife.

While they were eating Megan asked Chui Tewuh what he'd like to do in the United States.

"I would like to teach," Chui Tewuh said.

"It may be a little difficult," she said.

"Why?"

"Well, because you've got an accent," she said.

"What does that mean?"

"It means you speak English differently," she said.

"I see, I thought everyone spoke differently."

"Yah, but your accent is strong."

"Strong like what?"

"Strong like strong!"

"I see, but I've got a Masters degree," Chui Tewuh said.

"It doesn't matter. American children wouldn't understand you when you speak," Megan explained.

"Do you understand me when I speak?" Chui Tewuh asked.

"Yes, I do but I am struggling," Megan said.

"Struggling to do what?" Chui Tewuh asked.

"Struggling to understand you," she said, frowning.

"Oh well, why can't other Americans make an effort to understand me like you do?" he asked.

"They are impatient," Megan said.

"So the problem is not me; it is them," Chui Tewuh said.

"Maybe," she said.

"Do all Americans speak in the same way?" Chui Tewuh asked.

"No, we don't but we understand one another," she replied.

"There's some truth in what Megan is saying, Chui Tewuh. If you go into teaching you may face challenges because of where you come from," Luki cut in.

"What do you think I should do then?"

"Let's obtain a social security number for you first and we'll figure out something for you."

The following day Chui Tewuh and Luki went to the Social Security administration building to obtain a social security number. When the card arrived in the mail a week later, Luki advised his friend to swallow his pride and get a factory job to begin.

"You've got a wife and kids in Africa. You need to start putting some money away for their trip to the United States. Get what you can and see how things turn out," Luki said.

"I hear what you're saying, Bro," Chui Tewuh said.

"I know a fast food company which is hiring right now. Tomorrow I'll take you there to look for a job," Luki said.

"Thank you. What would I do in America without you?"

The next day Chui Tewuh accompanied Luki to Anchor Foods Products, Inc. where he was asked to take a test in English and math to be employed as a production associate. The same day he was told he had passed both tests and asked to go for a drug test.

"Massa, dis wuna kontry na helele-oh. Man don pass test finish dem say mek yi go do drug test, na who tell dem say me I de smoke banga?"[245] Tewuh complained.

"Bo, you don see wheti? Dis wan na daso di beginning. You want do seb mbambe wok dem go mek you write kan-kan test. Enter mek we go,"[246] Luki said, slamming the door of his merco[247] car.

"Ah, ah, massa!" Chui Tewuh exclaimed.

They drove to Concentra Occupational Health Services where Chui Tewuh was tested for drugs. The results mailed to him two weeks later showed he was drug-free.

The following day he started work at Anchor Foods. His shift ran from 10:00pm to 6:00am Monday through Sunday in a production line. He was required to wear steel-toe shoes, gloves, a hair-net, ear-plugs, and a white apron similar to the one won by nurses in hospitals. His friend bought these things for him because he had no money.

Anchor Foods was a beehive. In one corner of the building, some people stacked while others mixed flour. At the other end, some fork-lifted while others cleaned. Chui Tewuh's job consisted of packing appetizers into cardboard boxes for shipment to whole-sale companies throughout North America. The noise produced by the machines drove him insane. At times they were so fast that he couldn't keep pace. When this happened, team mates would yell, heaping racial slurs on him. One day, a team mate called him a black monkey who could not distinguish his right hand from his left. That was the last straw. Chui Tewuh ran straight into the office of the company manager and told him that he would commit manslaughter if people did not stop calling him bushman. It was only after the manager convened a meeting and emphasized the need for team spirit that associates stopped treating him like dirt.

"Massa, da wok na kanwa,"[248] he told his friend.

"You've got to be patient. Everyone who comes to America goes through this," Luki encouraged his friend.

"Is that true, bro?"

"Oh yes, I did worse things, including cleaning faeces from the buttocks of old senile white people in assisted living homes," Luki said.

"*Bo*, it's terrible! Can you imagine that the job is so tedious that I have to ask for permission from time to time to go to the restroom and rest? I just sit down on the toilet seat to breathe normally for a couple of minutes!" Chui Tewuh said, looking worn out.

"This is America, the land of dreams!"Luki said, a smirk on his face.

"My brother, even nightmares have limits!" Chui Tewuh retorted, wiping sweat from his broad forehead.

After working for six months Chui Tewuh rented his own apartment and started making arrangements to bring his wife and children to America. Tohnjeuh Natasha was now well and could travel to the United States. He thought it would be wise to obtain immigrant visas for them before buying air tickets.

An immigration lawyer to whom Chui Tewuh had presented the four cases advised him to file a Form I-130 titled 'Petition for Alien Relative'. He promptly did as instructed. After four weeks he received a letter from the Immigration and Naturalization Service requesting him to provide proof of paternity for his three children.

"My brother, proof of paternity na which one no?"[249] Chui Tewuh said, showing Luki the letter from the INS.

"Massa, I mimba say na wuna go big book?[250] Luki said, grinning.

"Massa, lef man da big book tory,"[251] Chui Tewuh said, wearing a look of frustration.

"Proof of paternity means that you have to do a DNA test to prove that you're father of your three kids," Luki explained.

"Which kan kontri be dis no? You don born pikin finish dem say mek you show say na you born'am? Barlok!"[252] Chui Tewuh said.

"This is America, land of the freed," Luki said, sympathizing with his friend.

Chui Tewuh and his friend did not know where to go for an immigration paternity test. After a painful search, they discovered a company called ReliaGene, a DNA laboratory and research facility based in Louisiana. Tewuh was asked to pay the outrageous sum of $ 3900.55 for the test. When he paid the money, ReliaGene sent a registered nurse to Chicago to take a blood sample from him. The company then sent a letter to Cameroon inviting Tohnjeuh Natasha and her three children to go to the American embassy in Yaoundé for blood samples to be taken from them. These were to be sent via diplomatic courier to the ReliaGene laboratories in Louisiana.

Six months had passed since the blood samples were taken from Chui Tewuh, his wife and kids. He hadn't heard from ReliaGene yet. Then one fine afternoon while he was eating lunch, the postman knocked on his door and gave him a priority mail labeled 'DNA results'. Fingers quaking, he opened the envelope and read its contents:

"Bitie Tewuh and Bunkwe Tewuh are biological offspring of Chui Tewuh and Tohnjeuh Natasha.Fongeh Tewuh, not biologically related to father."

Tewuh fell off his chair spilling the bowl of rice and pepper soup he was eating on his clothes.

"Papa God'eh! What have I done to you, hein?" He cried, rolling on the floor.

"*Cringgg! Cringgg! Cringgg!*" the phone rang.

"Hello!"

"Hello Chui Tewuh! Luki here."

"My brother, I have terrible news-oh. Please, come over if you can," Tewuh said, still weeping.

"What is the terrible news now?"

"Massa, I can't discuss this on the phone, come over quickly," he said, hanging up the phone.

When Luki arrived at his friend's flat, he was lying on the couch sobbing.

"What's the matter, Chui Tewuh?" Luki asked, shaking his friend vigorously.

"Massa, read this letter," he said, giving him the documents he had received from ReliaGene.

"Really, this is bad news," Luki said, throwing himself on the couch beside his friend.

"One of my children is biologically not mine! What does this mean?"

"It means that you are not the biological father of the kid. That's what it means," Luki said, shaking his head from right to left.

"In other words, my wife cheated on me?" Chui Tewuh asked, throwing his hands to his chest.

"Massa, how can you ask me if the earth is round?" Luki said.

"Well, this is the end of my marriage with Tohnjeuh Natasha," Chui Tewuh said, rising from the couch.

"So what are you going to do? Marry another woman?"

"Never! I'm done with women!"

"Are you going to bring your three kids to America?"

"Two, the third one is my wife's child."

"Oh, come on! A child is a child, born in or out of wedlock."

"That's not the issue."

"What's the issue?"

"The issue is breach of marital vow," Chui Tewuh said, wishing his friend goodnight.

The next day Chui Tewuh mailed two air tickets and a photocopy of the DNA results to his wife. He enclosed a hand-written letter in which he asked Tohnjeuh Natasha to send his two daughters to America and wished her a happy marriage with the father of her son.

NOTES

1 My friend, I am sure that with this kind of qualification you have, you will be a great person in this country.

2 Please, forget about his qualification, let's go and dance makossa and eat at home.

3 Mr. Tewuh, remember us when you are rich. You know that when your brother is on top of a plum tree you would eat the sweetest plum.

4 Sister, you are right.

5 Obili junction.

6 Your mother's vagina.

7 Carcass of a dog! Don't touch me!

8 Prostitutes.

9 Alcoholic beer.

10 Good for nothing person; fool.

11 To be.

12 Do you want a woman for the night?

13 No, my sister. I am not looking for a woman. I'm looking for my tribesman who lives in this city.

14 What is the name of your tribesman?

15 He comes from Meka village.

16 Are you from Meka too?

17 Yes, I hail from Meka.

18 I think I know the Londu you are looking for.

19 Is that true? So you know my tribesman!

20 Yes. Is Londu not a taxi-driver?

21 I don't know what he does for a living, sister.

22 My goodness! What kind of person are you? Are looking for some one you don't even know?

23 My sister, I have just arrived from Bamenda. I am in search of a job here. My father says when I get here I should look for Londu.

24 My friend, give me a bottle of beer. I will find Londu for you.

25 What do you drink, sister?

26 I drink nothing but 33 Export beer.

27 I'll be right back, my brother.

28 This is your tribesman.

29 Staple food made of corn flour.

30 Smoked tilapia

31 An unmarried man would starve to death if he couldn't cook.

32 May God save us!

33 Give a bribe.

34 Foolish Bamenda man.

35 Anglophone, English-speaking person.

36 Metonym for Cameroon.

37 Son of a bitch! Are you sick?

38 Anglophone! Get lost, idiot! Go tell your mother to carry you there!

³⁹Sir, I don't understand the dialect you're speaking.

⁴⁰Here is Yaoundé. You have to speak French, do you hear me? Here we speak only French.

⁴¹ What?

⁴² He is a Biafran.

⁴³ Yaoundé General Hospital.

⁴⁴ Are you sane?

⁴⁵An ideophone in the Bamunka language expressing great surprise.

⁴⁶ These are words of wisdom.

⁴⁷ Hat made of multicolored fabric won by men of title in the grassfields region of the Republic of Cameroon. It is painstakingly embroidered.

⁴⁸ We agree.

⁴⁹ Propitiation song intended to appease the ancestors.

⁵⁰ Traditional cup made out of the horn of a buffalo.

⁵¹ Mother.

⁵² Traditional outfit.

⁵³ A local deity.

⁵⁴Witches.

⁵⁵ Amulet.

⁵⁶ Lorry in a dilapidated state.

⁵⁷ Brothers and sisters. I greet you in the name of our Lord Jesus Christ.

⁵⁸ What sort of ill-luck is this? Who is Jesus, madam?

⁵⁹ You evil-doers, repent for the kingdom of God is at hand.

⁶⁰ There are all sorts of insane people on this earth.

⁶¹ Madam, what do you smoke?

⁶² She smokes marijuana.

⁶³ Spacious outfit worn by men.

⁶⁴ There is no problem.

⁶⁵ Abbreviation for brother.

⁶⁶ We are going to have it tough with them. All they do is steal money.

⁶⁷ They will all die one day. We are all mortal.

⁶⁸ They say a goat eats where it is tethered.

⁶⁹ It's you people who have been to big schools. You should write a letter to those people in Yaoundé.

⁷⁰ Trouble

⁷¹ My mother! And we call this our country?

⁷² Madam, human beings talk endlessly. This is not a Bible matter.

⁷³ My brothers, God's time is the best. Don't worry; we are all children of our Father in heaven.

⁷⁴ Don't worry. God is kind.

⁷⁵ Show the documents of your vehicle, driver.

⁷⁶ Here they are, chief.

⁷⁷ Where is the vehicle registration certificate?

⁷⁸ It's inside, chief. Here it is.

⁷⁹ Ha! Ha! Ha! It's expired. Its life has come to an end.

80 I did not understand the mixed language you spoke, chief.

81 I said your vehicle registration certificate has expired.

82 Which paper is called PeriMary, chief?

83 I said the life of your vehicle registration certificate has come to an end.

84 Oh hooo! I did not know chief. I will get a new one tomorrow.

85 I understand but you must give me some small thing now.

86 I don't have anything to give chief now. Let me go, I'll give you something on my way back.

87 What! What are you telling me?

88 This is my first load, chief. I don't have something to give you. Wait for me on my return trip.

89 Never! Give me something now; otherwise you will stay here until nightfall.

90 This is the way people from Small London behave. You're close-fisted. Please, give that thieving chief something and take us away.

91 Your mother's vagina.Who is that pompous fellow meddling in things that don't concern him?

92 It's me. Give money to that corrupt gendarme officer and take us away. Respect people who are above you.

93 Thanks so much. Many thanks.

94 How are you, my friend? I'm looking for my father who works here.

95 Who is your father, my friend?

96 He is Dr Bunkwe

97 What sort of work does he do, brother?

98 He is a divisional delegate, brother.

99 I think I know him. He is Doctor Cow, right?

100 Doctor Cow?

101 Yes, everyone in this town calls your father by that name.

102 Alright, do you know where he lives?

103 Yes, give me some small thing and I'll take you to his house.

104 Baggy

105 That's your father's home.

106 It's who you know that matters.

107 Paste made out of corn and steeped in red palm oil.

108 Paste made of fried groundnut mixed with fish and other condiments.

109 Illegally operated taxi.

110 Traditional sponge.

111 Witchdoctor's shrine.

112 My countrymen, I greet you.

113 We greet you too.

114 I have been working with you for one month now.

115 That's true.

116 I want to let you know that I am happy with the great job you are doing.

117 We thank you so much for the compliments.

118 And for the help you have been giving us.

119 I just want to let you know that I am here to help you. Let nobody hesitate to come see me when s/he has a problem. Do you understand me well?

120 Sir, we understand you very well.

121 A dead man is not afraid of the cemetery.

122 I know that a dead man is not afraid of the cemetery but we are not talking about death here.

123 Thank you sir, that's how rascals behave.

124 There is no problem, mother. Don't worry about them.

125 My office number is 666. It's open to you at all times. Let no one hesitate to come see me. Do you hear me?

126 Yes, sir, we hear you.

127 Are there any questions?

128 Mistresses

129 We are behind you, friend. Keep up the great job.

130 We work our asses off and all the bosses do is steal the money.

131 My son, help us put shame on their heads.

132 Do they know the word 'shame'? They are not ashamed. They can even trade their mothers for money.

133 Thank you so much. If you hear that I am dead, know it's because I am fighting on your behalf.

134 God will not allow that to happen. Keep up the good work; we are behind you.

135 Meeting.

136 Mr.Tewuh, this beer is given by your friends.

137 Many thanks to you, my friends; let God provide more.

138 Drink, friend, if it gets finished, we'll add more.

139 Thanks, my friends.

140 Who is this?

141 Please, pay me and let me leave this house peacefully.

142 Money for what?

143 What do you mean? Did I not spend the night with you? Please, give me the money. Sleep-overs are paid for.

144 Watch out! Please get out of this house peacefully.

145 Misfortune! Give me the money; otherwise I am not leaving this house.

146 Leave this house! Who brought you here in the first place?

147 Look at this foolish man from Praprakara! Do you bring a woman to your house when you know you don't have money? Trouble begets trouble.

148 Dirty prostitute leave this house. Did I have sex with you?

149 Whether or not you had sex with me, the issue is that I spent the night here. Give me the money.

150 Whores are thieves.

151 You are a thief, too. Look at this worthless man. Can you have sex? Since we came last night have you touched my inner wear?

152 That's because you are a whore. What business do I have with whores? Take this and leave this house with your ill-luck.

153 Ill-luck too, if that was intended to be an insult.

154 Native Sabbath.

155 Giant rat.

156 Juju or witcraft.

157 Bride.

158 Bride

159 Wine.

160 Some people behave as if they are superhuman.

161 Woman, are these your eyes. I missed you so much!

162 Quit bluffing. Did you look for me?

163 I looked for you in vain. You girls!

164 Tell me, where are you bouncing to?

165 I'm looking for beer to drink.

166 You are fond of beer.

167 Yeah, I can't live without beer.

168 Privately owned bar generally located in the owner's residence. Here they sell not only beer but also fried chicken, pork and, at times, fish.

169 Roast beef deliciously seasoned with red hot pepper, groundnut oil and other condiments.

170 A garment for the lower body that exposes the buttocks, consisting of a narrow strip of fabric that passes between the thighs supported by a waistband.

171 Secret society.

172 Some one who has lived in the Fon's palace for nine years serving as a royal page.

173 Group of the top-ranking elders in the village.

174 Oh my God! What sort of trouble is this?

175 You are scarcer than the urine of a cat.

176 My friend, we are together. How can we fix this problem?

177 White man.

178 Native of the grassfields of Cameroon

179 Pair of rubber slippers.

180 Celebrate a victory.

181 Police men.

182 Bald.

183 Privately owned student residences.

184 Fish.

185 Traditional bag for title holders.

186 Buffalo horn.

187 Traditional ceremony of asking for the hand of a girl in marriage.

188 Locally brewed wine.

189 Spacious men's outfit.
190 Spacious embroidered women's dress.
191 Market day.
192 Head of a slaughtered cow.
193 Locally distilled liquor.
194 Locally brewed beer.
195 Heavily embroidered cloth used in the grassfields of Cameroon by the royalty and title-holders.
196 Africans living overseas, especially in the United States of America and Europe.
197 How are you doing?
198 Here we are pal, nothing has changed.
199 Ah! Natasha, how are you, girl?
200 Your remark is out of place.
201 You are better off.
202 Blue-collar work.
203 This country is tough.
204 Problems; trouble.
205 How may I help you?
206 Sir, I don't understand the dialect you speak. If you don't speak French, there's nothing I can do about it.
207 A hat worn by notables.
208My son, give my own share of the money. Let me eat before death takes me away.
209 Aunt, this green card lottery that I have won is not money.
210 Ah! Ah! If lottery is not money, what is it? Please give my own share and let me leave peacefully.
211 Aunt, you're my mother. I can't lie to you. Lottery is only a sheet of paper given to me by the American government that allows me to enter the country.
212 Go away! You youngsters are full of tricks!
213 What are you going to eat in that distant land? Do they cook fufu and huckle-berry soup there?
214 No grandma. There is no fufu and huckle-berry soup there but we will not die of starvation. White people do not go to bed on an empty stomach. There is food there. We hear there's a lot of hamburger and hotdog in America.
215 Those people eat dogs!
216 Loincloth.
217 Amen
218 Delivery truck.
219 My friend, God has actually buttered your bread.
220 Brother, it's pure luck.
221 Cassava paste wrapped in banana leaves.
222 Sixth sense.

223 What sort of ill-luck is this?

224 I have no clue what's going on.

225 Chief: term of respect used when addressing police officers and gendarmes in Cameroon.

226 I don't care.

227 If you pay I'll let you go, but if you don't you'll stay here.

228 These whites are insane.

229 Fetish.

230 These whites are fools.

231 Brother, it's a long story. I'll tell you when we get to your home.

232 My friend, they say that my wife has contracted a disease called Africanosomiasis.

233 My friend, I've brought a small quantity of ndole for you. That will make you think of home.

234 My friend, isn't it better here than home?

235 We are only chatting. How can one compare Heaven and Hell?

236 My friend, is this the kind of wives you guys have here?

237 What do you mean?

238 How can a husband prepare food while his wife relaxes in the chair?

239 Brother, if you go to Rome do like the Romans.

240 My friend, I hear you but I don't think this type of marriage will last.

241 Whether or not it lasts, it doesn't matter to me. It's a marriage of convenience, contracted for the purpose of obtaining identity papers.

242 What is marriage of convenience, my brother?

243 I am referring to a marriage where you wed an American woman for the purpose of getting your green card very fast.

244 Oh, ho! I had been wondering about this matter.

245 Brother, this country of yours is tough. After passing the test they are now asking me to go for a drug test. Who told them I smoke marijuana?

246 My brother, you haven't seen anything yet, this is only the beginning. They make you take all sorts of tests even if you apply for a blue-collar job.

247 Mercedes car.

248 My friend, the job is tough.

249 My brother, what is this story about proof of paternity?

250 My friend, I thought you were one of those who went to institutions of higher learning.

251 My friend, stop talking about higher learning.

252 What kind of country is this? After fathering children they require you to prove that you are their biological father? This is unfortunate!